AN IMPOSSIBLE SITUATION:
OPPENHEIMER IN TIME

AN IMPOSSIBLE SITUATION

OPPENHEIMER IN TIME

LARA TIGLER, MD

PALMETTO
PUBLISHING
Charleston, SC
www.PalmettoPublishing.com

Paperback ISBN: 979-8-8229-2836-7
Hardcover ISBN: 979-8-8229-2907-4
eBook ISBN: 979-8-8229-2908-1

TABLE OF CONTENTS

A NICKEL IN TIME

Lara was walking in the street. There was very little traffic because all the adults were at work during the day. It was a quiet, residential street with stately trees and large homes set back on their lots with plenty of front yard landscaping. The summer day was a welcome change from the ferocious Chicagoland winters. School was out and all that was left to do was hang out and play with all the neighborhood kids.

Lara did not give the nanny much thought; she was probably getting lunch ready or doing some chores. But this was Lara's chance to run wild and seek adventure.

There was a nearby forest preserve and river; that was always a possibility. But the neighborhood playground was only one block away from her house, and that could be fun as well. As she was strolling toward the playground, she noticed that a tiny portion of the pavement in the street was worn down to such a degree that she could see the original brick that had paved the street decades ago. She went to get a closer look.

To her delight, she saw a shiny metal object. She looked around and saw no traffic on the road. The neighborhood was quiet and safe. So she bent down and stared at this gap in the pavement. She marveled that her street used to be paved with red bricks. How fascinating.

She could see that in between the bricks there was a small coin. She picked it up. It was a common, everyday nickel. There seemed to be no distinction between it and the coins that she used in present day. But when she looked even closer at the coin, she saw that it was dated 1905. She was so excited. She had a small coin collection, and this would be a nice addition.

As she stood up, she felt a bit of a head rush, but she also felt something else, nausea. That was strange. She knew that when you stand up too fast, sometimes you get a bit light headed, but she had never felt nausea before.

As she recovered and looked around, she noticed that all of the road was red brick. She also noticed that her clothes had changed. She was wearing a practical dress; it sure seemed to be an old style. Some neighborhood kids were walking toward her. They looked familiar, somewhat like her own neighborhood buddies. They had a ball, and they were heading toward a vacant lot, about one block away. With surprise she realized that that lot was located exactly where her modern-day playground ought to be.

Astutely she realized that she had traveled back in time. But she had no idea why and no idea how. The kids were very near her now, maybe only ten feet away.

One of the boys said, "Well, hello there. I have not seen you before. Are you new to the neighborhood?"

Lara answered, "No, I have lived here my whole life."

But of course she realized that this would be difficult to explain, so she added, "But my house is across Fifth Avenue."

"Oh, that explains it then. Do you want to come play ball with us?" he asked.

Naturally, Lara answered in the affirmative. As she walked with the other children, she attempted to make small talk. She said, "Is there anything that I can buy with this nickel?"

Immediately the same boy said, "Let me have a look at it."

He inspected the coin and said, "Oh yes, you can buy us something at the nickel and dime store down the street! We can share an ice cream soda or a large bag of candy."

All the children liked that idea. It was decided that they would play at the vacant lot first and then all go together to the store. As Lara was playing ball with the neighborhood children, she wondered why in the world she was transported back in time. Getting back to her own time did not seem to concern her in the least, at least not for now.

A girl in the group began to chat with Lara. With astonishment Lara realized that this was one of the daughters of a very nice family who used to live in her present-day home. As the girl talked, Lara gleaned that she was upset about her father's health. Even though Lara had learned about the name of the prior owners when she was a very small child, she did remember that their surname was Pointe. And she also remembered that the mother *and the father* had sold the property to her parents. She knew without a doubt that the father would live a very long life indeed; why, he must have been at least in his seventies or eighties when he had sold the home to her parents in the early 1970s.

The Pointes had had several children and greatly enjoyed their home. They were happy to sell to Lara's parents because they could see that another loving family would take care of the home, their family treasure.

Without thinking, Lara said, "Oh, your father will be all right. In fact, he is going to live a very long and happy life. You have a bright future. All will be well."

She saw the girl's face lighten, as if a heavy load had been lifted from her shoulders. To further lighten the mood, Lara said, "Do you want to hold my nickel?"

The girl forgot her sadness and said, "Sure."

As Lara passed the nickel to her new friend, she began to feel that same nausea as when she had originally found the nickel. Soon she realized that she was heading back to the future, to her home time. This time, though, she felt less ill and had the presence of mind to be aware of her time-travel journey. She felt light and peaceful. It was white and bright but not oppressively so. She felt as though she were in a cloud, only it was not damp at all. And she felt her clothes returning to their 1970s style. She was in the playground, and she was standing right where she had been in that vacant lot all those decades ago, back in the 1910s.

There were lots of kids around, and no one seemed to notice that Lara had shown up so suddenly. She began to play with her friends. Soon, the strange time-travel incident was out of her mind altogether. But she did have a strong feeling of déjà vu when one of her friends suggested that they all go to the gas station and get a treat.

As the gang of kids was walking past Lara's house, she saw that same worn area in the road that she had seen earlier that day. She remembered the nickel that she had found. She searched her pocket, and there was no nickel. She realized that she had returned that nickel to its proper time. Lara also realized that she had lightened a heavy load for her new, dear friend in the past.

Lara had no idea how she had traveled through time, but she was glad that she had done so. Somehow Lara knew that she had played a small role in reassuring that little girl, and maybe even Lara had returned the nickel to its rightful owner.

All was set right. Lara realized that the only thing she had left to do was drink a lemonade and get a treat from the gas station with her friends.

CHAPTER ONE

THE ASSASSIN

A beautiful woman was walking right toward Lara. In a flash Lara was reminded of that James Bond movie when Halle Berry's character came walking out of the ocean onto the beach that separated her and Bond. She was a sight to behold, pure loveliness (and perfection). Only this woman walking toward Lara was taller, and her bikini almost seemed armored. Astutely Lara saw a small knife in the woman's right hand, stealthily held by her person. Lara thought that the woman's slightly odd apparel must have concealed this weapon prior to the woman brandishing it.

But these observations were nearly instantaneous with another thought, one of preparation. Lara was no match for a trained assassin, but she did know how to act decisively, and that could make a difference. The woman's expression was angry and purposeful; Lara knew the woman wanted to kill her. She was still in the lounge chair as the woman approached, about to lunge, but Lara was able to swiftly lift her right leg and cross it over her left leg in order to kick hard on the assailant's wrist. This caused the woman to lose her grip on the knife, and in that brief moment of distraction, Lara lifted the stone mug that she had been using for her fruity drink and smashed it on the woman's head.

Quickly Lara changed position with the falling, and now unconscious, lady. Lara gently laid her down on the lounge chair and covered her head with the bottom side of her floppy sun hat. The now-incapacitated assassin was breathing nicely, a steady rhythm of soft and relaxed respiration. Lara was so relieved. But at the same time, Lara was disappointed because she knew that she may have to face this woman again in the future. But Lara was not about to kill anyone, not if she could help it. She needed time to think, so she sat on the beach right next to the unconscious criminal. Anyone now looking at the two women would just think that the two beauties were enjoying the beach just a little too much, with the decorative drink umbrella and the cherry now spilled onto the sand.

Moments before the assassin had approached Lara, she had had an intuition that the $250,000 in her bank account was about to be stolen. It was a feeling of multiple hunters closing in on her; she just knew that she was being watched and that the wolves were closing in. Lara now remembered that just before the woman came at her, she was about to lock her bank account. Without hesitation Lara did just that. She realized that her quick reaction to the assailant must have been observed by someone, and that that someone could be in cahoots with the assassin. She also thought that if the assassin did have an accomplice, then it was possible that that person was counting on time to be able to breach her account. Thanks to Lara's intuition, and the ability to act with conviction, whoever was trying to steal from Lara was thwarted.

However, that meant that she might still be in danger. Now she had to think of how to get off the beach without being captured. She had no enemies, but she was a military spouse. Lara knew that a few years ago, the Office of Personnel for the military was hacked. She had gotten a notice from the federal government about it. She also knew that just two years ago, in the year 2020, Russia had successfully breached nearly *all* government digital records, hers included.

Lara's husband was away on a mission. She knew it was top secret and need to know only. But could her husband somehow be making some very powerful people mad? She knew that she had just spoken with him, and she knew that her children were in a secret place with relatives. For now the only thing on her mind was escape.

CHAPTER TWO

THE BIKINI

It took so many years to realize that she had superpowers. In fact, it was in watching her boys' favorite show, *Wild Kratts*, on PBS, that she was finally able to verbalize that fact. Chris and Martin Kratt teach children all about animals in this excellent TV series. Almost in every episode, they mention that the creature that they are highlighting that week has "creature powers." For example, the flamingo can sleep while standing on only one leg. The snow hare has such big feet in order to walk over the snow without sinking in it, kind of like natural snowshoes. Lara began to realize that for all of her life she too had special gifts or powers. Just as all rabbits and hares do not have big feet adapted to the snow, Lara had gifts that not all humans possess.

One of her superpowers was clairvoyance; she could literally close her eyes and see what was happening around her in the world, even if it was happening in a faraway place. She could even see a bit into the future. Lara was still sitting on the beach next to the unconscious assassin. With practiced ease, she drifted into a calm, centered place. Lara created a still lake in her body and all around her body. She saw daylight, and it was a pleasant place. It was quiet.

Lara gently suggested to the stillness, please show me what is behind this attack on me. Lara breathed with intention and calm, patiently waiting for the answer that she knew would come. She saw a hidden place deep underground. It was on the East Coast. The word *Virginia* popped into her head. Lara remained still; she wanted more information and was hoping it would come. She saw a large, thick metal door. A white light was beaming under the door. Somehow Lara knew that this was part of the United States military complex.

Lara was stunned. Could a fellow American be her enemy? She had to find out.

A man was approaching Lara; it broke her out of her trance. He looked at ease and had a casual walk. But Lara was unsure of who to trust. She saw a crowd of young volleyball players nearby. Quickly she got up from the sand and brushed herself off. As she fluffed her hair and fixed her bikini, she decided to join that group and shimmy off the beach toward the tiki bar nearby. She donned her skirt and went straight to the crowd. She pushed her way into the center of the players, and when they walked near the bar, she darted outward into the group of people who were happily imbibing on the beach. She saw a sign that said "Restroom" and went straight to it.

Luckily the medical conference she had attended was finished. She had already gotten all her credit, and these last couple days were to be icing on the cake to this wonderful "working" vacation. Her tiny purse held her identification, money, and passport. All she had to do was get to the airport and take the next flight and she would be safe at home in Kansas. Again Lara calmed her nerves. She saw the layout of the resort hotel in her mind's eye. There was only one main road to the airport. A shuttle bus should be coming any moment to take guests to the airport. As she was thinking this, she saw a shuttle out the restroom window. She had a couple minutes. If she could dash to that bus and successfully get on, then she would be one step closer to getting to the United States without hassle. She was pretty sure she could use a credit card at the ticket counter. Well, here goes, she thought.

She casually walked out of the restroom. There was a man looking intently at her. This was her cue to run. As she ramped up her escape, she saw that same man in her peripheral vision get up from his table. He was going to make a pursuit. Adrenaline rushed through Lara's brain but not surprise. Her intuition had never failed her, and she was prepared. Now she ran at top speed. The bus was just one hundred feet away. The tropical foliage was luxurious in the backdrop of her drama.

She could feel a tug on her bikini top. Really? Who would do such a thing? She wiggled and he lost his grip. She did a little dance side to side and joined the line waiting for the bus. Everyone could see the people waiting for the bus, and the man decided not to make a scene. When she looked all around, he was gone. Lara gave a sigh of relief. Now her next challenge was navigating the airport without incident. She had to conceive a plan.

CHAPTER THREE

FIRST CLASS

As soon as the bus started to move, Lara felt a sense of relief. She could sit and relax, even if for just a few minutes. She soon realized that her attire was entirely too casual to be headed to the airport. It looked rather odd not to have a purse and a suitcase, not to mention wearing a bikini top, short skirt, and flip flops. Well, it was not the end of the world to have to buy new things.

As she looked around, she noticed no familiar faces and no suspicious stares. She was glad for her spontaneity in catching this bus. She wondered how and when she would be able to see her family again and whether she should contact them right away. Thinking about it, she realized that she had a bit of time. Best to focus on the task at hand, and that was to successfully and safely return to the United States.

As the bus rounded the airport and was heading for her terminal, she began to look around. She really could not discern anything amiss in the area. She would go straight to the ticket counter and try to have her ticket changed to an earlier date. If she could only get through security safely, she thought, it was highly unlikely she would be followed past the TSA checkpoint. But what did she know?

To Lara's delight there was a flight home, and it was leaving in just ninety minutes. Perfect. When the ticket agent called her over, she explained that she wanted to take this earlier flight. The ticket agent told Lara that there were a few seats on the airplane but only in first class.

He asked Lara, "Is that all right?"

"Are you sure there are no coach seats available?" she replied.

Something in the way he looked at her was a little off, but he said, "Double checking, no, not a one."

"First class it is," said Lara.

As she finished her transaction with the ticket agent, she felt certain that she was somehow manipulated to be placed in a certain seat on the plane. Probably someone just wanted to keep an eye on her? she wondered. Whatever was going on, she did not like it, but she knew that she had to trust her instincts. She left the ticket counter and headed straight for security. The guard gave Lara a look over and she could tell he disapproved of her attire, but at the same time, he seemed to appreciate it as well. Whatever his thoughts, he let Lara pass through the scanner as though it were the most normal thing in the world to see a passenger with nearly no clothes on.

Now Lara was in her element; she loved shopping. Lara was too practical to shop for anything that she did not really need, and she tended to buy items that were more of a classic style rather than trendy, so she really did not shop too often. So this unexpected opportunity gave Lara a much-needed boost to her low morale.

She decided to splurge and buy makeup and accessories as well. One trip to the nearby restroom and Lara felt like a new woman. Normally she would love the chance to delve into a new book from the airport, but Lara knew there was no way she was going to have that kind of concentration while on the plane. Instead she perused the magazines and bought two, one about parenting and the other about housekeeping. Light reading but useful at the same time, why not?

She chose a seat as close to the entrance of the gate as possible. A single lady sat right next to Lara and gave her a friendly smile. After a while Lara thought of something. Why not ask this lady if she wanted to trade seats? Lara began to make small talk. Turns out this lady was also a physician, and she was leaving the conference right on time in order to get home to her family as soon as possible. Once they developed a good rapport, Lara decided this was the right time to ask the lady about switching seats.

"Hey, they bumped me up to a first-class ticket, but I really do not want to sit that close to the door. Would you like to switch places with me? Where is your seat in the plane?" Lara said hopefully.

"Oh, wow, that is so very kind of you. Are you sure?" she replied.

"Yes, absolutely, it was the airline who bumped me up. I never asked for that seat." Lara was so relieved.

"Well, all right then. Great," she replied.

The two ladies were talking like old friends. They even bore a bit of a resemblance to one another. They decided to risk it and actually exchange boarding passes. That way the very first flight attendant who saw their ticket would be in agreement with the flight attendants on the plane as to the owner of the respective tickets, and they would be less likely to be bothered.

When the time came to board the plane, their plan went over without a hitch. Lara's new friend boarded first, naturally. When Lara passed her friend, heading toward the coach area in the back of the plane, she was sure she saw a scolding look on the face of her friend's seatmate. Lara did think of confronting this man, but she thought that that might not be at all helpful and might only antagonize him. If he wanted to chat with Lara, he certainly knew where to find her.

The flight went smoothly, and Lara took a much-needed nap. Plus she did not know what awaited her on the other end of this airplane journey, so she had better reserve her energy for a fight-or-flight response just in case.

Once the seatbelt sign went off, Lara reached for her seatbelt to undo it. Just as she began releasing her seatbelt, she felt a bit of nausea and everything around her went white, like a misty cloud. Once the cloud cleared, she found herself on an entirely different plane. It was a smaller plane, and it looked quite old. Lara found that her clothes had changed; she was wearing a sort of business dress suit and she was carrying a briefcase. The other passengers were dressed in a formal style as well, but they were all men. Strangely none of the men commented on her sudden and unexpected appearance on the plane. They were all intent on exiting and so Lara followed suit. She did get a fair number of sideways glances, and she could tell the men were admiring her beauty; they were well pleased for the distraction to an otherwise dull day.

The flight attendant ushered everyone out of the plane and asked them to please head toward the baggage claim area. Once inside Lara realized that it was not only the plane that seemed stuck back in time but the entire airport also looked like a scene from the 1950s. Once again Lara found herself transported through time. She had experienced this kind of time travel before, and she believed that it was God sending her on some sort of assignment. The few times she did travel through time, it always seemed to be for the purpose of setting a little thing right. Like that one time when she was a child and she had returned a lost coin to a girl who lived in her neighborhood decades in the past.

Lara was none too pleased to be in the past. She was eager to get back to her own time and try to set things right there. But she was certainly not in control of this adventure, so she decided to just go with it. Why God should elect to treat her on a need-to-know basis rather than just plainly telling her about what is really going on was a mystery, and to be honest, it was quite frustrating as well.

A man approached Lara and said, "Hello, young lady. Are you the secretary that I sent for?"

Lara managed to give him a smile and the slightest of nods.

"Wonderful. I am eager to get to work. Do you have any bags?"

He was friendly and helpful, she thought.

"Uh, no. No, I don't," she replied.

"Even better. Follow me," he said as he began walking toward a limousine.

Once inside the luxurious vehicle, Lara began to see why this adventure might serve a purpose in her own time. There were two gentlemen sitting in the spacious limousine, and they both had military uniforms on. Was it possible this trip back in time had something to do with her current mystery? She would soon find out.

CHAPTER FOUR

ATOMIC BOMB

O ne of the military men said, "Mr. Oppenheimer, this matter is classified. We have not properly vetted your new secretary."

J. Robert replied, "This matter is urgent. She is here to take notes. I can vouch for her discretion."

"Of course," the man replied.

Lara was stunned to hear the name Oppenheimer. She had a vague recollection that this man had something to do with the making of the world's first atomic bomb. At Albert Einstein's urging in 1939, President Roosevelt had formed the Manhattan Project. Numerous scientists worked on the development and testing of the atomic bomb. The first mushroom cloud appeared over New Mexico on July 16, 1945.

Without thinking Lara opened her briefcase and took out her notepad and pencil. With alacrity she made her pencil ready. Oppenheimer was speaking, and without effort or concentration, she saw her hand move over the notepad with astonishing speed. She recognized the shorthand that she was writing from her days as a Girl Scout in the 1970s. Lara had learned Morse code, sign language, and shorthand, among other skills, while participating in her Scout groups.

The conversation between the three men continued in a surprisingly banal direction until she heard the words "alien technology" and "the ability to nudge humans into following either the devil's bidding or obeying the word of God."

What? Lara momentarily paused at her task. One look from Professor Oppenheimer made her return to her duty as a scribe. One of the men was explaining that technology would have to advance quite a bit before they (Lara wondered who *they* were) would be able to pull something like that off.

Fortunately, at that moment, something outside of the limousine drew the men's attention. Lara had to think fast. The word *nudge* nagged at her. She recalled that only a few months ago, in her time of course, in the year 2022, she had heard an interview on NPR about nudge theory. She had gotten the impression that this was a recent development in human scientific understanding. The book was titled *Nudge: Improving Decisions about Health, Wealth, and Happiness*, and one of the authors, Richard H. Thaler, explained the term in the context of economics. Lara thought that was a far cry from having any cosmic impact or touching on theology in any way.

Apparently Thaler had developed the theory in the year 2008. Basically it explained how to nudge people to make decisions that can be difficult but benefit them in the long term. He mentioned that an individual or group can be given all the options, and they are truly free to make any choice that they would like to make. But one option might be put forward with a nudge, and these individuals or groups would more than likely take the decision that was presented with a nudge. Thaler won the Nobel Prize for this work.

Lara had been curious enough about this interview that she had looked up nudge theory. To her surprise the concept of nudging someone to make a certain decision could be useful in more areas of human experience than just the economy. Just give someone positive reinforcement of some kind and indirect suggestions (think subliminal), and one could have an influence over that someone in the areas of political theory and behavioral sciences. Being a family physician, Lara's curiosity had been piqued.

Even in Lara's time, it was beginning to be understood that it was indeed possible to achieve an interface between the human mind and artificial intelligence. If humans could be nudged to make a certain decision from an influence that was outside of their minds, then how much easier would it be to nudge them from inside of their minds? Maybe that is what the men were referring to when they were talking about the need to develop technology in order to achieve this manipulation on the human mind, and apparently also the soul.

Her attention was drawn back to the conversation as the men resumed their deliberations. Dutifully she recorded every word.

The same man spoke and said, "The only souls not affected by this influence are those that have been saved. They seem firmly fixed to God's kingdom. It is almost as if they are part of God himself; they just cannot be nudged."

"And aren't there souls that are fixed to the devil as well?" the other man asked.

"You can't really believe all this nonsense about heaven and hell and a cosmic battle between good and evil, can you?" said the professor. "We have just got to stay focused on this bad element within our ranks. The military-industrial complex is strong. President Eisenhower warned us about this potential danger, that the military-industrial complex might outstrip the powers that be. Now on to another subject, please."

Turning to Lara, the professor said, "Give me the notes on this last part of the conversation."

Lara did as she was told. She tore them out of her notebook and saw the professor tuck them away into a very slim slit in the book cover of his Bible. In that moment she wondered why in the world he carried around a Bible if he did not believe in God. But then she thought, people often say one thing and truly believe another thing. Perhaps this professor was keener than he let on.

In that very moment, Lara felt herself return to that whitish cloud, and she knew that her time in the past was over. Her own time was about to come into focus.

CHAPTER FIVE

A PASSENGER DIES

It seemed that nearly all the passengers had taken off their seatbelts, but there was a delay in getting off the plane for some reason. In a way that was a blessing because Lara was still reeling from her time-travel experience; she was grateful to be back in her own proper time.

She sat in her coach seat and pondered. It had taken her decades to even realize that God does indeed send us through time, and not just in a linear fashion. She came to realize that God uses time as a tool to help the drama of the cosmos play out. For God, time did not really exist; he was present in all times. He was the master of his servant, time.

Lara always wondered why he sent her on time-travel excursions. She came to understand that these brief excursions were always for the good and never for the bad. It took her a while to become accustomed to the adventures, but once she did, she almost enjoyed them. They gave her a perspective on her own life and how important every soul's spiritual journey is to them, but also to the entire cosmos. It was gratifying to see how the pieces of the cosmic puzzle fit in just their right spot, a spot that occupied time and space, but also eternity.

For example, she had come to understand that something as simple as a lie can make a tear in the fabric of time and space. The universe is made of truth and love and nothing else. When someone lies, it ignites an explosion of anti-truth, like antimatter, and the mess, the vacuum of that explosion, has to be repaired. It has to be made right. Someone has to repair that rip, and as you can imagine, almost always it is not the liar who volunteers for the task!

But this current adventure back in time did not appear to be that simple. In this recent time-travel excursion, she was more like a witness than a fixer. She recalled what the gentlemen were talking about; they were insinuating that advanced technology already existed in other worlds, alien worlds, that may be used as a weapon against souls, a way to manipulate an individual but also the masses. She realized that using artificial intelligence to manipulate souls' decisions could create much more than a tiny rip in space-time!

She recalled that one of the military men had mentioned that saved souls were immune to the influence of this artificial intelligence weapon. In a thunderclap she realized how she could be useful to God! She realized that she herself was already saved; that must be why God was involving Lara in this mystery. She could be of use, but it remained to be seen exactly how.

She also realized that someone, somewhere, had pegged her as an enemy. Clearly that someone knew about Lara's salvation status, if not also her superpowers. She had lived her life in a discrete manner. How she had shown up on somebody's radar was a mystery in and of itself. She was a doctor and an author. She was also a military spouse. But nothing that she had done or written about was particularly controversial. Well, there were too many unanswered questions. She had best get off the plane, get home, and make a plan.

As she went past the first-class seats, she saw that one person had stayed behind. He had a cane. Clearly he was just taking his time to depart the plane. Lara asked, "What happened? Why were we delayed?"

With a sad expression, he answered, "Don't you know? One of the passengers died."

Shocked, Lara asked, "Was it a man? Was he sitting right there?" as she pointed to the seat where she knew the angry man had been seated.

"Sadly, yes, it was him," he answered as Lara was practically pushed from behind to depart the plane. But she knew who it was who had died. She just did not know why.

CHAPTER SIX

BURNER PHONE

Once Lara arrived in Kansas, she felt an incredible sense of relief. All the dangers and adventures that she had had in just the past twenty-four hours seemed like a dream. A weird dream at that. She brushed it all off and summoned a rideshare. The trip home was uneventful. On the way home, she made a call to her five-star hotel in the Caribbean islands. She explained that she had dropped off her key card properly, but she had left all her belongings in her room due to an unexpected emergency. She would like them packed and sent express to her home in Kansas. The concierge readily agreed and explained that the charge would be added to her bill.

That done, the next call was to her husband. To Lara's delight, he answered the phone on the first ring; she was so glad to hear his voice.

"My love, I'm headed home. I mailed you a care package with your favorite beef jerky." Beef jerky was their code word for danger. It was a signal that they had to talk on their burner phones.

"I'll be glad to pick that up for sure, love you," her husband signaled back. Lara knew he would call her burner phone in about twenty minutes or so. Perfect.

"I love you too," she replied as she hung up the phone.

Lara reflected about all the many security features that her husband had insisted that the family adopt. More than once their family's high level of vigilance had come in handy, in ways that were unpredictable. This current situation being a case in point. She never imagined a time when they would need to use their burner phones. It was just a precaution; she never thought they would use them.

As the vehicle pulled up to her house, she gave the usual pleasantries and flashed the driver a warm smile. Lara prided herself on her excellent driver feedback and wanted to keep her high rating; even that could come in handy one day.

Entering the home required Lara to pass several layers of security. Hidden cameras scanned the outside perimeter of the home. She knew her face was being scanned. Her husband could access their smart home technology to watch her every move; Lara was counting on it. At the front door, her eyes were scanned as she spoke a simple sentence to allow for voice recognition as well. She typed in a simple password so that the computer could scan her fingerprints. If any of these biometric tests failed, then she would not be allowed access into the home.

If anyone was observing her, they might simply think that there was a password needed to enter the home. Lara could be speaking on her phone when she was prompting the voice recognition software; that would not be unusual. In this way the high level of technology that her home contained would not be readily apparent to the average person.

If there was a bad guy or rogue actor in the military-industrial complex, it did not follow that that person or persons could easily breach her home's defenses. Maybe when that assassin was approaching Lara, it was to take her hostage and obtain some biometric data. Maybe all of Lara's defenses were still intact.

In any case, Lara knew that panicking was useless. She had gotten this far in her life, and her faith told her that all was well and that all would be well. She had been in hellish situations before, and she had always come out on the other end. It was not really correct to frame it as God was on her side. She had come so far spiritually that she had finally realized that in reality there are no sides. Once she had become saved, she had become a spiritual master. The Holy Mysteries were opened to Lara, and nothing was as it had appeared before her salvation experience.

The uncertainty and doubt that so many human beings suffered under was a thing of the past for Lara.

In that old paradigm of life as suffering, life and death seemed pretty straightforward and inevitable, if not also incredibly burdensome. But once Lara became saved, she realized that death really is the last enemy to be overcome. She realized that everything Jesus ever said was actually true. It is just that things looked mightily different from a heavenly point of view!

However, Lara was not blind to the possible worldly dangers that a mystery like this could bring to her family. She had to be shrewd.

Her burner phone rang. It startled Lara into more practical thinking. "Hello," she said eagerly.

"Talk to me. Tell me your situation," her husband ordered.

Lara explained the violent incident on the beach. She told her husband about her wolf intuition and explained that she had successfully locked their bank account. She recounted her rapid escape from the islands and her safe arrival in the States. And she told her husband about the dead man and her time-travel experience.

"Impossible," he said.

She replied, "Which part?" But the phone went dead before she could hear his answer. Reception was notoriously bad with overseas military calls. She would try to call him back in a few minutes. But she wondered, which situation was impossible? What could her husband mean?

CHAPTER SEVEN

TIMING

Her cell phone rang before Lara had a chance to think through the possibilities of impossibilities. Mind-blowing stuff.

"Hello," she said after she pressed accept on her cell phone and made sure to click on the speaker option so that she could be hands-free. Lara had come to realize that Bluetooth headsets were a waste of time for her. Either they got lost or they got broken, and she was constantly having to manage her various and sundry Bluetooth purchases. Nice idea, she thought, but with twin infants and then twin toddlers, she came to realize that she had way too much going on. If she was with her boys and they needed quiet, then she simply did not bring the cell phone into the same room with them. Sometimes she would turn down all the volume on the phone. In the first few years of rearing her children, this got to be quite hectic, but recently she found a physician job that had no after-hours call (that means patients can call you day and night outside of normal business hours) and she had a great nanny, so her life had become simpler and less stressful.

"Hello. My name is Candy Trix. I am a producer at Netflix. I have had a chance to read your book *You're Saved*. We have had a lot of success with our *Lucifer* series, and we think we can do the same with your spiritual memoir. I am just touching base to see if this is something that might interest you."

Lara was elated. She had envisioned just such a possibility. Her first book, *You're Saved*, was based on her life story, but Lara knew that it could easily be embellished and segmented in order to become a TV series of sorts. After Lara wrote it, she had a feeling that the book resembled the TV series *Medium*, which came out in the mid-2000s and ran for seven seasons, and *Lucifer*, which was a Netflix series that also ran for several seasons and initially came out in 2016.

Lara knew from real life experience that both Father and Mother God existed. She knew that angels really did play an active role in managing God's plan here on earth. She knew there was a devil, and she knew that the human drama was really a cosmic one, just as the TV series *Lucifer* depicts. She knew that the Bible stories really did have some historical fact behind the creative writings, as unbelievable as some of the Bible stories are. And just as in the *Medium* TV series, she knew that she, too, had a connection to heaven, and for some reason she was given paranormal gifts, although she was only human, that helped her manage or make right difficulties here on earth. The protagonist in *Medium* was a woman with psychic powers; her name was Allison DuBois. Amazingly Allison DuBois was a real person, not just a TV-show character. Her heroism in helping the local district attorney's office solve crime was remarkable enough to spawn this successful TV series/drama.

At the same time, Lara could not help but wonder about the timing of the Netflix offer. Time. More and more it seemed, everything was coming down to time for her. It was beginning to dawn on Lara that God was grooming her as a time traveler. It was only once Lara had become saved that she began to see the intricacies of time. At the moment of her salvation experience, she instantly felt that she was saved for *all time*. That included her past, the past when she had been lost. She knew somehow that her past had changed, and it had changed for the *good*.

She had marveled that her past could actually be *changed*. It was just as the book of Revelation in the Bible had said, "He will wipe every tear from their eyes. There will be no more death or mourning or crying or pain, for the old order of things has passed away" (Rev. 21:4, New International Version).

She now knew that this quote from the Bible was not talking about the future. It was not reassuring us that one day we would have some sort of relief from our pain. It was not that. It was actually talking about the here and now. It was talking about what it meant to live *outside of time*, to live in God's kingdom for all eternity. "The old order of things has passed away," or in other words, that old paradigm of time would no longer serve.

How uncanny, Lara thought. Before she was saved, she had no idea that being saved would bring her into a whole new perspective on the cosmos. She had no idea that time was a tool. A tool that God used to bring out the truth, and ultimately, to set us free. Jesus said, "And ye shall know the truth, and the truth shall make you free" (John 8:32 King James Version). Jesus lived as a man, through time (all the stages of human experience: infanthood, childhood, and manhood), to show us the path to complete obedience under God, and ultimately, to save us *for all time*.

But she had to answer this producer's question. She said, "I am interested, yes." Lara was keen to hear what this Netflix producer had to say. She realized that taking her book "live," so to speak, would bring her to a wider audience, and she wondered if that bad actor in the military-industrial complex would be watching.

CHAPTER EIGHT

FAMILY MEAL

After Lara hung up the phone with the producer, she had a lot to do. Her children were on their way home. More than once Lara thought with gratitude about her parents-in-law. They were always so generous with their time. She knew her twin boys had had a wonderful time out west camping with them. Of course they were not so into roughing it really. A nice cabin at the campsite, along with the occasional restaurant sit-down meal, was as far as they went in terms of doing without. But Lara's boys loved all the attention, and the constant recreation of using the pool and playing at the playground were really all that they had hoped for. Lara's husband, Adam, was the one who showed the boys how to fish and all the necessary survival skills. The twins would just have to wait for their favorite hobby of fishing until their dad came back from Europe.

Lara put aside any thoughts about aliens and cosmic conspiracies. She was not even worried about her husband. She knew he could take care of himself. Thoughts of Professor Oppenheimer intruded a bit. She wondered about his life. But research on that would just have to wait. She got to straightening up the house. She made a kid-friendly dinner that consisted of Kraft mac 'n' cheese, fruit on the side, and of course steamed broccoli with ketchup on the side. The boys would be thrilled. Lara had just changed from Minute Maid juice boxes to Honest Kids. The apple juice tasted out of this world delicious. She would give each boy two juice boxes of their favorite brand.

But what to do for her parents-in-law? Quickly, she grabbed a family meal out of the freezer. All she had to do was stir occasionally for about thirteen minutes and her parents-in-law would have a hearty and healthy meal.

Lara listened to the news as she prepared their dinners. It all seemed bad, and violent. But nothing really stood out for her. She could hear a car pulling up in the driveway. It must be her family. Lara looked at the smart monitor in her kitchen. It was her oh-so-adorable kids. Oh, what joy! Lara always looked forward to seeing them after they were apart. She rushed to the front door to let them all in.

"Papa, Grandma, boys!" she said as she moved to greet them all. Papa always gave the best hugs. And Lara had come to learn that her mother-in-law, although slow to warm up to anyone, had the deepest affection in her hugs. But when Lara came to hug the boys, it was like a pack of friendly dogs pounding and licking all at once. Somehow or other, Lara and the boys ended up on the floor in a great big sleep pile, as they liked to call it. Finally all the uproar diminished. Everyone said how hungry they all were.

Lara got to serving everyone a dinner dish, and they all sat down to say the usual family prayer. It was short but heartfelt and then everyone dug in.

Papa was the first to come up for air, "How was your medical conference?"

Lara knew this was her cue to thank him for taking the boys for a week. She said, "Oh, it was very productive but also difficult. I learned a lot, especially at the end." That was as far as she felt comfortable telling her parents-in-law about her extraordinary experiences. Over the years, she realized that few people could take in the enormity of some of her supernatural and mystical experiences. Truth be told, she was only gradually understanding them herself. But she continued, "Thank you so much for watching the boys. It means a lot to me."

Gratified, he went on, "It was our pleasure, although I have some bruising that will take time to heal. That is for sure."

Lara knew what he meant. Grandpa was particularly physical with the boys. She had learned from her husband that her father-in-law was physically abused when he was a child. She knew that he had abused her husband somewhat as well. Although, to his credit, he really did try over the years to break away from that sort of upbringing. He knew that Lara and Adam never even spanked their kids. And that omission was not because her kids were not naughty sometimes. Far from it. But Lara and Adam knew the research showed that that type of parenting was futile and even harmful to the children. They just had to dig in and find the love and patience necessary to find another way. It was an ongoing process of trying to be a better person, a better parent.

It was a Saturday. Her parents-in-law would stay overnight and then fly back home to Virginia early in the morning. That would leave most of Sunday for Lara to get the boys ready for returning to school on Monday and hopefully also try to get all her own ducks in a row as well.

Her father-in-law, Papa, she liked to call him, surprised her with a comment, "I got a hold of Adam a bit ago. He told me to tell you that he won Professor Oppenheimer's Bible at an auction in Europe. I didn't know you guys were collecting historical Bibles. That is so interesting. How shocking to put religion and the first atomic bomb in the same man. I guess that is a collectible!"

So many thoughts went through Lara's mind. It did not surprise her that her husband had acted so quickly and that he had saved the day (or might have saved the day) by obtaining some sort of clue to their present cosmic or alien mystery. She was eager to get her hands on that Bible, and it was not necessarily to read a favorite scripture! She wondered if it was the same Bible from her time-travel experience. And she also wondered what else the professor might have hidden in the book cover.

"Well, if we are starting a historical Bible collection, I believe Hubby has found our first relic," Lara said with pride and a smile. Her father-in-law also smiled. She knew he was retired military. Lara also knew that her father-in-law, Papa, was a working member of the military-industrial complex. But she knew it was a sprawling organization. She quickly wondered, If there was a rogue player in the institution, how high up was he (or she) in the ranks? Could her Papa help solve this new mystery or could he in some way hinder their progress? She was not sure. Time would tell. She almost laughed out loud at her unintentional joke. Thankfully, she hid her amusement in the nick of time. Gosh, there she went again. Time. It was all coming down to time.

CHAPTER NINE

ALIEN BEACH

Lara said one last goodbye to her dear parents-in-law, and then she and the twins enjoyed waiting for a bit and guessing which plane was theirs while watching planes taxi down the runway. It had been so enjoyable to attend church with them earlier that morning. Lara could not help thinking how grateful she was for Sunday school. She was able to sit in the pew, in the nave (the central part of a church building where most of the congregation sits), relax, and enjoy the beauty of the church architecture and art. But of course, today, she had the extra pleasure of sitting with family. What a joy it is to pray and worship with loved ones. One of the great highlights of this life to be sure!

Once she and the boys were all buckled in their respective seats, and the air conditioner was on full blast, the excitement began anew. The boys knew that today was special; they would have Mom all to themselves, and she would spoil them and love them.

"Where to?" Lara asked the twins. "What shall we do today?"

Isaiah was the first to respond. "Let's do something different. Something we have never done."

"Let's go to the beach!" said Jacob enthusiastically. Lara had just returned from the beach. The assassin's approach was vivid in her memory, but she did not let the boys see any fear on her face.

"Let's do that!" Even though they lived in Kansas, Lara was up for the game of imagination and pretend.

Instantly, upon agreeing to play pretend beach with the boys, Lara felt the now familiar whitish cloud overtake her senses. The nausea was only ever so slight. She could almost hear her children laughing with delight. What could they be thinking about this unique experience?

When the air cleared, she found herself standing on a white-sanded beach. It seemed to go on forever. Immediately, Lara had a sense that her vision was sharper here. In her own world, she should have been able to see about three miles to the horizon. In this new world, it felt as though she could see much farther. She wondered what that could possibly mean in terms of this planet's size. She noticed two suns, or should she say stars? They were yellow. She knew that this time (there she went again, no pun intended), she had traveled through space, not just through time.

The air was cool and fresh. No one else was present, except her two sons! They were laughing, and almost in unison, they said, "Where are we, Mom?"

"I don't know, babies." She liked to call them babies. But they were precocious, independent little boys now, not really babies. Lara's mind always flashed to one of her favorite movies, *Independence Day*, when she told her boys she did not know something. She loved the dog scene where the mother figure (the girl-friend of Will Smith's character) answered her son honestly that she did not know something when disaster struck. It was just the honesty the little kid needed, and the mother held him tight, so that was all that really mattered.

The three of them looked around, trying to get their bearings. It felt so peaceful. None of them felt any anxiety whatsoever, which was odd considering their surroundings. But they all realized that they had gotten their wish: they were at the beach! Just not a beach that they had ever imagined or seen in any movie.

Isaiah said, "Well, we are at the beach and it is different."

The three laughed. Yes, it was different indeed!

They saw a white light off in the distance. It was hovering and it was shaped almost like a sphere. It was slowly making its way toward them. And what was remarkable was that it was hovering over the ocean, and the ocean was the color purple. It was then that they realized that the sky looked somewhat purplish as well.

And the trees, as beautiful as they were, were not green. The trees looked golden. But it was the whitish ball coming toward them that captivated their attention; they could not keep their eyes off it. They realized that the ball was not very large. It was just that their vision was so much sharper in this world that the ball looked large in the faraway distance.

The white ball landed next to them on the beach, and it turned into a lady. She was dressed in a long, white robe. Her hair was a rich brown. Her face was beautiful. She looked almost human, but there was such a kindness in her facial expression that the person she resembled the most, here on earth, was a hospital nurse leaning down toward you asking what she can do to relieve your pain. She was that good.

"Hello, dear friends, welcome." Her voice was like a song. Her English was impeccable.

Lara replied, "Hello. This place is completely unfamiliar to us. Can you tell us where we are? And why we are here?"

"Of course, dear one. You are on a planet far from your own. You have begun your space travels, your training in traveling through space, not just time."

Somehow Lara understood that this lady knew what she was talking about. After all, the lady already knew that Lara was an amateur time traveler. But in all the time-travel experiences Lara had had, she had never met someone who knew who she really was. Yet this lady knew her.

"How do you know me? And why are my kids permitted to travel with me? Are they training to become travelers for God as well?"

"Your children have not yet formed themselves; it is unclear what they will choose as their final assignment in eternity. They are here because you are their mother and they are saved, just as you are saved. God gives the gift of travel to whom he will." She spoke with patience and wisdom. Lara wondered what else this lady knew.

"I have only just begun to realize that *I am* a time traveler for God. Isn't it a bit early to move me to the next level?" Lara said only half-jokingly.

It was obvious that the lady perceived much more than Lara's words; she could empathize with Lara as well. There was an emotional connection between the two women and the children.

"You are a mystic traveler." The lady spoke as if it should have been obvious. All at once, a flood of understanding came over Lara. On earth, she never really had anyone to talk to about her spiritual gifts. Life on earth was so chaotic, so much was going on. It was difficult just to keep your head above water in that other world, in her world (Lara began to realize that not only did she have sharper vision in this world, but she also had a whole new perspective on earth as well; it was just one world out of many now). But here and now, in this new world, she saw her mystical training as clearly as she saw the ocean in front of her. She realized that she was a mystic Christian. How uncanny that she had to travel to another world, probably far away in another galaxy, just to realize who she was!

Laughing, Lara said, "People in my country don't exactly have a positive view of Christians nowadays, and now I am supposed to be a die-hard Christian *and* a mystic traveler!" It was great the Creator of the universe had so much faith in Lara, how flattering. But it was unclear how she was supposed to navigate her life with this new information.

As if right on cue, the lady said, "All is well and all will be well. We have lots planned for your enjoyment and enlightenment here, both for you and your children. Come with me and let us begin." And she held out her hand, expecting Lara and the children to take hold of it. Without hesitation, they did just that. All their hands joined together like a football team holds hands before a game. It was a way of signifying that they were all ready for what lay ahead, and they were all ready to win!

CHAPTER TEN

MYSTIC TRAVELER

Lara and the kids woke up feeling refreshed and ready for anything. The angel-like lady (technically an alien) had brought them to their lodging yesterday. To their surprise, they had been terribly hungry and sleepy. The lady, along with a few of her friends, had been an attentive host. They had shown them a table, and on that table was a scrumptious feast. The food was not anything that Lara and her boys had ever eaten before. It was a simple matter of dishing whatever looked good on their plates. And it all looked good!

To their delight, the food had tasted as good as it looked. There had been something like pizza and something like BBQ ribs. There had been deliciously spiced vegetables, or at least foods that sure seemed as though they were vegetables. The beverages were full of flavor and made you feel that your thirst had been thoroughly quenched. And the boys had enjoyed something that seemed very much like ice cream. It was cold and creamy, anyway.

The light had gradually dimmed. It was unclear whether that was by design or due to the natural rhythm of the two suns. But after eating, it was obvious that they really needed to be shown their sleeping quarters. To their relief, the hostess brought all three of them to the same room. It was quite spacious, and everyone had their own bed. There was a bathroom for Lara and a separate restroom for the boys. They had everything they needed. Fresh bedclothes had been laid out on each bed. To their amazement, they were the exact style and coloring that each of them had desired.

Lara's mind flashed to the *Star Trek* TV series. Her favorite one was *Star Trek: Voyager*. She remembered that there were many times when Captain Janeway was hosted by aliens on their planet. This experience felt eerily similar. Only Lara knew that, rather than the Federation sending Captain Janeway to planets far, far away, she had been sent here by God. She was on a mission, apparently a training mission. And unbelievably, her sons had been allowed to accompany her on this fantastic trip.

She had recalled that the angel-like lady had explained that they were all able to come together because they were all saved. Having her salvation experience had been life altering. But when it had happened, all those many years ago, Lara had seen it in the context of her Christian religion and her earthly life.

Slowly, over time, Lara was learning, was mastering, the Holy Mysteries. Even before she came to this planet, Lara was beginning to understand that salvation was a step in her earthly life, to be sure, but it was also a step in her *cosmic* life. She was coming to understand that Christianity was only a small step in the many steps that she would be taking in her journey to commune with the Creator, whom she called God, or the Holy Trinity.

Jesus had been her gateway to salvation. Being a Christian was the best choice she had ever made. She knew that Jesus had come to earth to save the lost and give us the truth. But she was coming to understand that the other major religions on earth could also be useful for obtaining salvation. Jesus had come to save all humankind, but he was not particular about which religion we chose. He just wanted us to be true, to *want* to return to God's kingdom. He wanted to make sure we understood that there is no shortcut to salvation. We really do have to repent and *want* to return to the Creator; it is as simple as that. The best way to study and learn these truths is through participation in and the practicing of a religion.

With this budding understanding, Lara felt excitement for her eternal assignment as a mystic traveler. She knew that God would give her a choice as to how she spent her eternity, and she knew that staying in heaven was an option. She had always been one who was up for adventure. Traveling and meeting new people was her forte. Being a physician, she also felt she had a healing touch. Why not put these gifts together into one job? Well, if traveling the universe and making the crooked places straight was something that God thought she would be good at, then she was up to the challenge.

When she and the boys awoke, they really did look forward to the new day. And Lara thought she had a bit of an idea of what was expected of her.

There was a gentle knock at the door. Isaiah went to answer it. As he opened the door, a warm, white light flooded the room. It was not overpowering, but it did make them all feel as though they had just been given a cup of energy to drink.

The angel-lady, whose name was Aravia, said, "Good morning, dear ones. I trust you are feeling well?"

"Yes, very. Thank you so much," said Lara.

"We will start by taking the boys to their play area. Lara, you will always have the option to join them there. Also, periodically throughout the day, you will be sent a picture in your mind of what they are doing now." Lara understood that her gift of clairvoyance would come in handy here. Aravia must have known her spiritual gifts. Lara was relieved.

The group walked, almost floated, to a large outdoor meadow. The boys enthusiastically yelped for joy. There was an elaborate playground, and there were many children playing on the equipment. Isaiah and Jacob looked at Lara for approval. Lara smiled and they were off running. She would not see them again until the evening later that day.

"All will be well," said Aravia. And Lara knew that all would be well.

Aravia no longer used words. She looked at Lara and held out her hand. Without thinking, Lara grasped her guide's hand, and instantly they were enclosed in a white bubble of sorts. The bubble lifted off the ground. They were moving up and away from the playground.

It was not long before Lara saw an enormous stadium. The stadium was down below and coming up fast. It was impossible to determine how many people were in the immense crowd. Aravia made Lara understand that she would be joining the earthling section. Lara was stunned. There were other people from earth here? But Lara quickly realized that of course she was not the only one. Of course there were others. Apparently many others.

In a flash, Lara recalled a dream that she had had in residency. She was in a large stadium, and she was directed to the section where Martin Luther King Jr. was in charge. She felt immediately comfortable because he was her hero. In the dream, Lara was made to understand that she was beneath Martin Luther King and that King was beneath Jesus (Jesus was the main instructor for everyone in the stadium, and there were many other sections in the stadium, with many other believers). When she had awakened that next morning, she had only thought that she was being given reassurance that she was on the right spiritual track. But now, having had many time-travel experiences since that dream, Lara was beginning to realize that the dream may have served many more purposes than just spiritual reassurance. It might have been a precursor of what was to come.

The stadium below her seemed very similar to the stadium in her dream, only much larger. Lara wondered who would be in charge of the earthling section. As if in answer to her question, she noticed that one person in the section that Aravia had pointed out was more distinct. She recognized who it was, and she was not at all surprised to see that it was her Lord and Savior, Jesus Christ, waving her into their section and welcoming her to her first space-travel class.

CHAPTER ELEVEN

ARAVIA'S PLANET

Lara was overcome to meet Jesus here. She and the boys had only arrived yesterday. Space travel was completely new to Lara, not to mention to her two children. They had been taking so much in, it just never occurred to Lara that she would have such a direct, mystical experience while doing her space-travel training. All of her time-travel experiences on earth had been more along the lines of simply completing a task. The transition from her own time to the new time was always somewhat mystical, but it was very brief.

Lara had to be quick on her feet, literally. Jesus was showing her to her seat in the stadium. He gave her a broad smile, the warmest possible greeting, and then he disappeared down the aisle.

Lara sat down, as directed by her Lord. Before she could process this singular interaction with Jesus, her attention was drawn to the main stage at one end of the rectangular/oval-like stadium. A being, whom she could hardly describe other than to say he must have been a very large person, began speaking. His voice was melodic and clear. She understood him to be speaking in English.

What was strange about that, though, was that Lara quickly realized that the being had to be speaking in multiple languages. Or perhaps each person in the stadium could hear him in their own language somehow. The reason she understood this to be true was because as she looked around her, she saw her fellow earthlings. And from their varied dress and appearance, she perceived that they were from all four corners of the globe.

Immediately to her left was a woman whose dress and appearance meant it was likely that she was from China. Just to her right was a woman whose appearance gave Lara the impression that she was from Latin America. As she looked around her section, she noticed that there were thousands of people from earth sitting alongside her. She intuitively understood that they were not all Christians, at least not in practice back on earth. But she also realized that Jesus had saved them nonetheless. How fascinating and how telling.

Soon the being, the master of ceremonies, began reaching a crescendo pitch in his speech. Clearly, he was introducing somebody very important.

"And without further ado, I give you our Lord and Savior, the reason for the season, the pièce de résistance, the one and only Jeeeeesus Chrissstttt!" he said with all the usual fanfare of an excellent and celebratory introduction.

The roar of the crowd was unmatched in her experience. She knew that bull sperm whales could make the loudest sound of any animal on earth, 230 or so decibels of sonic boom, and a very loud human was able to yell up to one hundred decibels, but she wondered whether some of these alien species had abilities of sound that far outmatched even the bull sperm whales. Yet she realized that even her sense of hearing was enhanced in this world. Somehow she was able to withstand this tremendous cacophony.

As Jesus walked, or floated, across the stage and took his place at the microphone, Lara realized in a flash that Jesus was not only her section leader, but he was also the charismatic leader of the *entire* cosmic audience! She was completely taken aback. She had always wondered whether Jesus was the savior of just her world or of the entire universe or of some smaller subset of the universe, such as a galaxy or two, and now she got her answer. At the very least, Jesus was revered by people or beings from *many* planets, not just hers.

Again, she hardly had time to take this in when Jesus began talking. He had a natural charm and opened his speech with a joke. Nearly the entire audience guffawed for that one. Being new, she just did not get it. But soon he was transitioning to business of sorts. He began to talk about the newcomers who had just arrived. He introduced several people and he pointed to the section of the stadium where they were each seated. As he stated their name and a little about them, a whitish glow would hover over them, and it was quite a simple matter to see the person that he was introducing. Lara knew that much more than language was being used to convey his meaning. As he spoke about each newcomer, Lara was able to empathize with that person and almost see their entire life history in a flash before her eyes. The nearest Lara could relate to such an experience was what she had heard about end-of-life reviews at a person's death. Apparently, God would review the entire life of a person and help that soul understand how they treated others around them and what others had *felt* about how they had been treated. God would help that soul understand the lessons learned in that life and how they could have done better.

Of course this was only hearsay. Lara never thought in a million years that she would be able to confirm that something like an end-of-life review was possible. Yet here she was, reviewing someone *else's* life. She now knew that it was indeed possible to experience a life review and one did not necessarily need to wait until one had died to experience it!

And then Lara heard her own name called out by Jesus Christ. "And from earth, let's welcome Lara Tigler. She had no faith as a child, and then as a teenager Father God called her. And she answered that call!" The crowd exploded in applause. "It took her twenty long years, but she made it. She returned to God's kingdom with all of her heart, soul, mind, and strength. Let's give her a warm welcome!"

Once the introduction had been made, Lara experienced the white light given from Jesus and the full empathy from the crowd. Before that introduction, she had thought that she was getting an adequate understanding of the varied peoples here in the stadium, that she was learning about her Milky Way galaxy just by using the gift of empathy. But once the crowd's energy was fixed on her and her alone, she felt an amplified influx of knowledge of beings from all over the star system.

Then Jesus shifted to the main gist of his speech. To Lara's surprise, the "class" turned out mostly to be a comedy show. He was truly gifted at his comic timing. With each new joke, there was almost a wave of people in the audience laughing and reacting. Soon Lara began to see that this wave really did exist, and in a purposeful form. Jesus was playing the crowd, like a master plays the violin. The laughter and response from the crowd began to take on a melody of sorts, a dancing movement. His performance was nearing a firework-like display of magnificence in its finale.

Once the show ended, there was a final uproar of appreciative applause. Of course there was an encore, and then another encore. It was a star-studded show (pun intended), one to remember for all time.

The show had not taken that long, so Lara was shocked when she finally exited the stadium; clearly the day was nearing its end. Aravia was right on time to pick up Lara, and she gracefully flew Lara back to the same playground where her kids had been dropped off at the beginning of the day. Isaiah and Jacob spotted their mother and gleefully separated themselves from the playing group. They were running toward Lara but it was quite a long way. Lara took this moment to speak with Aravia.

But Aravia got the first word. "Your time here is over. You have done well on your first visit. The boys too."

"But I have not done anything! I have not learned anything about space travel. And haven't the boys only been playing and enjoying themselves all day? How can our time here be over?" Lara said exasperatedly.

Laughing, Aravia replied, "It's not about time really. Besides, time is a bit different here. This is not heaven. We are not living in eternity here. We are in your same universe, and we are governed by the same natural laws as your planet. It is just that things here are never as they appear. You will understand more when you return. For now, Jesus gave you exactly what you need, an introduction. And a spectacular one at that!"

Lara knew that Aravia was right. What did she expect anyway? A space shuttle and a space suit?

"I did learn a lot about beings from other planets and about what Christianity looks like in a broader, cosmic sense. But how will I know when to initiate space travel? And how can I do it on my own? I don't even have control over my time-travel experiences yet." Lara had so many questions. But the boys had just reached her, and they all embraced with affection and enthusiasm.

Lara and the boys began to feel that all-too-familiar whitish cloud, but Lara could still hear Aravia speaking. She was saying, "You will know, Lara. Keep to the narrow gate, 'because straight is the gate, and narrow is the way, which leadeth unto life, and few there be that find it'" (Matt. 7:13–14, King James Version).

In the next moment, Lara found herself in her truck, along with her boys, in exactly the same position as the one they were in when they were whisked away on their space-travel journey. Lara glanced at the clock on the dashboard display. It showed the exact same time as when she had asked the boys what they had wanted to do today. They had wanted to go to the beach. And what a beach it was!

But even though they had spent some time on that new planet, no time had been lost, no time at all. Yet Lara knew that they had just had the time of their lives!

CHAPTER TWELVE

THE DEVIL

Oddly Isaiah and Jacob did not seem too keen to ask questions about their space-travel journey. Lara did not want to press. The boys seemed content to just watch some cartoons; it had been a long day. It was time to relax.

Lara felt it was safe to leave them alone for a bit. She walked to her bedroom and lay down on her beautiful bed, no husband by her side. She missed Adam so much. She decided now was the perfect moment to call him again. If he had been able to connect to her father-in-law, then maybe Lara would have some luck as well.

"Hello," he said, after he answered the phone on the first ring.

Lara was ecstatic; she loved hearing his voice. "My love, I miss you so bad." She did not want to give too many details away on the phone, but she still wanted to let her husband know that she had learned about his auction purchase from her father-in-law. "Do you have the book?" She meant Oppenheimer's Bible of course. She was hoping he would pick up on her enigmatic style.

"Yes, we can add it to our collection." They did not have a Bible collection, but she got the hint that he was well aware that this matter was sensitive.

"Okay, great. I went to a beach with the boys; it was out of this world. And it took no time at all." Lara knew that her husband was used to hearing about her time-travel experiences. It would be a simple matter for him to figure out what she meant.

"Wow, I never would have expected a beach in Kansas." This time he laughed. It was so good to hear him make a joke!

"Have *you* been to a beach lately?" It was Lara's way of asking him how he was, an open-ended question really. He knew that she wanted to know every detail of what he was up to, but he also knew it was safer to tell her nothing at all.

"I wish," he replied. She got the impression from the tone in his voice that all was as it usually was, too little sleep and too little time to get all of his tasks and duties completed. It would be an endless effort to get the mission accomplished, and the officers would bear an incredible burden to see the mission through until the end. "I miss you too," he whispered.

Her heart broke. He needed her and there was no way for her to get to him. Or was there? "My love, are you at work or in your living quarters?"

"I just took a shower; I was about to go to bed." How many times had they wished that she could just teleport to him while he was deployed? Just spend a few hours cuddling together on his bed. All they wanted to do was touch one another. And then Lara could go back to the civilian world, he could go back to his work, and they would have both been a bit more refreshed and better able to bear the burden of war.

"Don't hang up the phone, babe, no matter what; give me a moment." Did he guess she was up to something supernatural? She could not know. But they had been married long enough, and he was trusting enough, so it just might work. After all, she had just learned that she was a mystic traveler. Surely God would not think it selfish of her to take a trip to Europe to see her beloved spouse, especially since a Bible had inspired the idea. She chuckled. It was funny to her, but probably because she was nervous. She had never initiated a time- or space-travel experience on her own before. She really needed to make sure her kids were all right. This had to work.

Quickly she grabbed one of her husband's small knives from his nightstand. She needed a good tool if she was going to look inside that book cover! She was eager to see if the shorthand notes were inside the book jacket. Probably she would need tape too. She would have to put the Bible back together again! It had to be seamless. Adam would need to bring that relic back home and it could not look at all suspicious.

She hurried down the stairs. The boys were still sitting in front of the television. They were laughing and looking intently at the cartoon. Lara passed them by and skirted into the kitchen. Luckily, she had just baked some banana bread. It was not often, but every now and then the twins did not eat the bananas before they went bad. And in anticipation of her parents-in-law's visit, she had baked blueberry muffins. There was only one left, but Lara knew that Hubby would much appreciate it!

She yelled out to the living room from the kitchen, "I love you boys!"

"We love you too, Mom," they said without taking their eyes off the TV.

Lara stood in the middle of the kitchen floor. With practiced ease she silenced her mind. She gently laid all clutter aside. She reached into her purse and fingered the small crucifix that she always carried. Her mind's eye was presented with many doors. They seemed countless. It was a beautiful place, light and peaceful. At first glance, she seemed alone in this new place. She looked to her right and saw a garden.

The garden was lush and green. It had a sense of mystery and opacity. It did not seem as though people traveled through it much at all. She looked closer. There was something like a white picket fence surrounding the garden. And if you looked even closer, there was a gate. The vegetation had grown up to such a degree that it hung over the gate, and the opening to the rest of the garden was very narrow.

As Lara was pondering this strange gate, a stranger appeared. He did not look at all pleased. His expression was sour, his stance fixed. "You are not welcome here," he groaned. His voice was familiar somehow. In a flash, Lara recognized him. It was the devil.

"I know you. You used to torment me! For no reason at all." She was still a bit resentful that she had had to put up with him for God knows how long! She was not blaming God really, but the two went hand in hand. Giving credit where credit was due, however, Lara had to acknowledge that it was only with God's help that she was finally able to free herself from the devil's evil intrusion into her soul. She recalled with disgust the easy access that the devil had had to her innermost being. It was her confrontation with the devil *after* her salvation experience that underscored the urgency of helping others to become saved. It was only when she *was* saved that she even knew that salvation was possible for her, and *necessary*.

"You can't banish me here. I can come and go. And I will not let you pass," the devil said.

Lara had to think fast. She knew that time travel was possible. She also knew that God had shown her that instantaneous space travel was possible too. What had Aravia said? "You will know, Lara...narrow gate..." It was a good thing Aravia had emphasized these words, and repeating them using the Bible as a context was helpful too. Lara realized that without Aravia's help, she might not have passed this test. But Aravia had helped her, and Lara knew what to do.

As she spoke to the devil, she felt like one of the little billy goats Gruff talking to the troll near the river. Her children's nursery rhymes would reassure her that this troll of a devil could be outwitted. "You cannot stop me from going through that gate. God wants me to be happy."

Without any hesitation, the devil neatly stepped aside. He was helpless to stop her. Lara walked calmly to the gate. She found the latch and walked through. Immediately, she sensed that same whitish cloud that she had always experienced in her time travels. The mist faded, and there was her husband lying in his bed, holding the phone, talking to *her*!

"I'm here, my love, I'm here!" Lara practically fell on top of her husband, and she began kissing him all over.

Lara felt his arms tighten around her. He was in happy shock. He knew what she had accomplished and he knew what it meant.

CHAPTER THIRTEEN

EUROPE

When people say, "Count your blessings," it always seems so cliché. Not that there had not been times when Lara hadn't wanted to count her blessings. When a move went smoothly, or a medical checkup gave good results, or a child was born with all ten toes, these were all times when it was natural to feel blessed.

But in regard to instantaneous space travel, both Lara and Adam never once thought it would be possible in their lifetimes. Since they were both scientists at heart (an oxymoron to be sure), whenever they contemplated traveling at the speed of light, or faster, they always thought it would be due to a feat of science. And obviously, in the current state of affairs, that sort of speed was not possible.

Once again, though, God threw them for a loop. First it was time, and now it was space. He had flung

Lara from Kansas to Europe within a fraction of a nanosecond, or less. All these years, when she had the occasional time-travel experience, she had only gradually learned to appreciate them and gain wisdom. But now, with these recent space-travel experiences, first the one to Aravia's planet and now this trip to see her husband, she was struck with the immensity of space travel. She was blessed!

It took a while for Adam to find his voice. Holding Lara was a dream. He loved when she would lie on top of him like a blanket. He felt her kissing him all over and his mind shut off. Desire overcame him. Soon he and Lara were intertwined in a hot, sweaty mess. It hardly mattered, the how and why of it. But after a long while, when they were both thoroughly satiated, they lay in his bed just staring and breathing. It was then that Adam said, "You came."

Chuckling, Lara nodded vehemently. "If it weren't for my experience with Aravia and her planet, I wouldn't have had the confidence to come. I guess I really did have some space-travel training after all."

"Wow. All these years, your time-travel experiences felt almost unreal. Surreal is a better word. I always believed you when you told me about them, but the stories almost seemed like a dream. I wonder, do you think God had multiple reasons to send you here? I mean, of course he wants us to figure out the Oppenheimer mystery, but do you think maybe he knew that I needed proof? Proof about instantaneous space travel but also proof about time travel as well?"

"I guess you already know the answer to those questions." Lara chuckled again, "And he knew just how to arrange it so that you would for sure remember the proof!" This time they both laughed, he while tickling her and Lara while begging for him to stop.

"I wonder how much time we have. Are the boys going to be okay?" He was worried.

Lara wondered that herself. She knew the twins were tired from their big day. But it was probably wise to complete the Bible task. "It's too bad we don't have time to really research his life. But I do think it best to look inside that Bible cover."

"Me too," he agreed.

Lara gave her husband the knife options that she had brought. He also greatly appreciated the baked goods and stashed those away for later. He chose a small knife and gave the rest back to Lara. "Can you keep that knife, my love?" Lara asked. If that was the right knife for the job, she wanted Adam to keep it just in case. He would be the main guardian of Oppenheimer's Bible. He might find something else about the Bible that needed a closer look.

"No problem. It was military issue anyway."

He went to his luggage and searched for the Bible. He brought out a parcel-like package. Lara mused, "This is so exciting. Maybe just the proof I need too! If my shorthand notes are in the book cover, then I will have physical proof of my time journey in that limousine." Lara did not need proof really, but she did want a satisfactory resolution of that mysterious interaction with the military men and the professor.

They held their breath as Adam unwrapped his purchase. He revealed an old-looking Bible. It was in good condition, but obviously well used. It was a King James Version, Lara's favorite. Adam opened the book to its title page, then flipped a page or two, and they saw the name *Oppenheimer* written in cursive as the owner:

The Oppenheimer Family

"Apparently, the ownership of the Bible has been verified. Not only that, but the auctioneer also said that this particular Bible has the desired provenance to date its origin back to the early nineteenth century in Germany."

Lara replied, "I would have guessed Professor Oppenheimer to have German Jewish ancestry, but that would have been just a guess. Maybe his family's religious history is more complicated than I had thought."

"Maybe the professor is like you. Not many people know that you completed the Jewish conversion process. For almost two years you practiced two religions. Who does that?" Adam said with obvious pride.

"Professor Oppenheimer?" They both laughed. "But seriously, I did not complete the conversion process, remember? Rabbi Coen did not feel comfortable presenting me to the elders for the mikvah bath because I believed that Jesus Christ is the messiah."

Adam clarified, "I know. But you did all the necessary work. You studied the Hebrew language, attended religious classes, and attended weekly services."

He did not have to remind her. She would have enjoyed her crowning moment before the elders. It did seem rather harsh that she was denied the natural culmination of her achievements in her mastery of Judaism. But it was precisely that denial that further informed her understanding of religious history, not to mention religious schisms. In the first century of Christianity, the followers of Jesus were mostly Jewish Christians. It is unclear why, but over time, Jewish and Christian worshippers separated themselves into two distinct religions. Lara was a product of that separation.

Adam was inspecting the Bible. "Where did the professor slip in the notes?"

"It was the inside front cover, I'm sure," she said confidently.

He was pressing his fingers on the inside of the book. "I do feel a bit of a bulge. But the pattern on the inside cover is almost textured and has a complicated design. I can see where it might be easy to hide a slip of paper in there." He held the knife in his right hand and began to slowly and systematically cut a slit in the very top of the book. He opened one inch and then another; pretty soon the top was open. The moment of truth had arrived.

"I think you should check it out, Lara; your fingers are more delicate than mine. I might rip it." He knew she was good with her hands. How many times had she removed a tick from his back when they had been hiking in the woods? Or taken out wooden splinters? Her skills had come in handy too many times to count.

She remembered the professor inserting the notes into the book. She could almost reverse engineer his movements in her mind. She gently inserted her right index finger into the newly made slit. She felt a piece of paper. She pushed her finger down past the paper and gently applied a shearing pressure upward. The sheet of paper moved upward; it was visible above the top of the book now.

They gasped. It was shorthand cursive on old paper. Jackpot!

"Let's make sure," Lara said. She removed the entire paper. It was the notes in shorthand. They had found the professor's Bible! Adam read the notes with Lara's help. He was amazed to have this window into the past.

Adam said, "Let's check the entire book, just in case." He made sure to check every inch of the book. He found another bulge. They looked at each other. They had to know. Adam made another slit. Lara felt inside.

"I feel another piece of paper jammed inside." She applied the same technique and removed the mysterious paper.

"I thought the professor did not recognize you as Lara?" Adam said confusedly as he looked at the greeting at the top of the strange note.

Dear Lara, I don't have much time. You left before I could explain. You need to give the word. Don't forget. Give the word. Family name.

The Professor

"Give the word? And what does he mean that you left? How could he recognize you?" Adam was still confused.

"He was not explaining anything to me in that limousine. The last thing he said to the military men was a warning, that President Eisenhower had warned us not to give the military-industrial complex too much power," Lara expounded.

"Do you think when he says 'word,' he means a password? Or God's word? But it seems like he means his name, Oppenheimer," Adam was guessing.

"I have no idea, my love. But I can feel our time here is done. God's pulling me away," Lara cried out.

Adam begged, "Please, no. Please stay." But it was too late. Lara was gone, and he was left with a broken Bible in his lonely room.

CHAPTER FOURTEEN

THE INTERVIEW

When Lara reappeared in her kitchen, she found herself crying. How could God separate them? Why was it so sudden? Hot tears fell down her cheeks. Her eyes began to sting. She wondered how her husband was faring. He, too, had to feel the devastation of such an acute loss. But Lara was not one to give in to self-pity. She knew that she had to pull it together. Just in the nick of time, too (it was always about time), she could hear Jacob calling out for Mommy.

Lara glanced at the stove-top clock. No time had passed at all. So it was a space- *and* time-travel experience. She wondered if her husband had lost any time or whether time had passed just as it normally did when they were together. But Jacob was calling.

"Mommy, I want some peas and carrots. And SpaghettiOs." He was so good at food prep details; it was only a matter of time before he was completely independent in that area. And he was only six!

"I'm starting it now!" Lara answered. She did not want to invite him into the kitchen this time; she wanted some alone time. Luckily, he was interested in the show on the television.

"Thanks, Mommy." Really, he was the sweetest child. She sure hoped he stayed that way.

"Isaiah, would you like hot dog SpaghettiOs?" It was worth trying. Although Isaiah was a bit pickier (he did not like the beef meatballs, but the Franko's were all right), he really did have a sufficient range of food preferences. There was always a chance he would say yes.

Isaiah looked away from the TV for a moment. "Okay, Mom."

Great. This evening's dinner would be easy. Although Isaiah did not like the peas and carrots, it was a simple matter to heat up the green beans for him. Once she was done making the dinner, she dished up the plates and spoiled them by letting them eat in the living room while watching TV. She had done this before, so the boys were not suspicious that she had not insisted on them eating at the dining room table.

Lara made a veggie cauliflower pizza for herself and joined the twins in the living room. They said a prayer and began eating. She started making a mental list of all the remarkable events that had happened to her in the past few days. She knew that God was playing a role in "assigning" her to this mystery and giving her helpful insights as to how to go about solving it. She also realized that Oppenheimer seemed central to the mystery. Her father-in-law worked within the military-industrial complex. Perhaps he could be a helpful resource.

As miraculous as God's interventions had been, Lara could not help but be a bit frustrated at God's lack of forthrightness. She knew that somehow, almost always, God was testing her at the same time as he was helping her to solve this mystery. She was not sure what to ask her father-in-law, at least not yet, so she decided to focus on Oppenheimer. The boys were still eating. They were laughing at the cartoon they were watching.

Lara went to Amazon's website and looked up books about Oppenheimer. She saw several good options. She used her search engine to read about which books were considered high quality. Normally, she would try to purchase books at a brick-and-mortar store, but she wanted to get these books as soon as possible. She went back to Amazon and bought a few books for her Kindle.

The download was nearly instantaneous. Still, her boys were happily occupied. She got busy reading the books on her Kindle at a rapid pace. She took notes in a paper notebook. Lara worked quickly. Reading biographies was one of her favorite hobbies; it would have been nice to linger and enjoy the literature. When she got to the interview when Oppenheimer was showing remorse for having helped create the atomic bomb, she read slowly. He certainly seemed changed. He grasped, perhaps more than most people, the dangers that nuclear bombs posed for the entire human race and the planet.

She wondered if, perhaps, his remorse was greater because he was already aware of the alien danger. Did he know of a plot against the human race? Did he know a particular person, or persons, in the military-industrial complex who might be a culprit in the diabolical scheme?

Not knowing why, Lara switched to YouTube. She wanted to see Oppenheimer's interview for herself. Maybe there was a clue in the video that she could not grasp in the biographies. Oppenheimer appeared sad. He was looking directly at the camera. She was not sure why, but she had a feeling he was looking directly at her.

"What is it, Professor? What could you be trying to tell me?" She focused on the man, his eyes. Were they blue? Were they brown? She leaned in.

She felt the familiar whitish cloud, and she realized that she was being transported through time and space to the TV studio where he was just finishing his interview. Lara looked down at her clothes; she was dressed in an appropriate outfit for the period. It was 1965. She was standing with the TV crew, and it appeared to her that they all accepted her presence as a matter of course. Maybe they thought she was a member of the crew.

Professor Oppenheimer had just finished. She heard the director say, "That's a wrap." Everyone in the studio seemed speechless. No one moved. Lara had compassion for the professor. She moved first.

She confidently walked up to Oppenheimer and gently said, "May I escort you to a quiet room? You can freshen up and take a moment."

He readily agreed. He seemed stunned, saddened. Lara searched her mind; she calmed her spirit. She was listening for the Holy Spirit's guidance. Surely he would help her give comfort to this stricken man. She saw the door that led out of the studio. She walked in that direction all the while listening inwardly. With gratitude she heard that same still, small voice.

"Right." It was almost always the same; he would use minimal words. It seemed that conversing with God was on a need-to-know basis. But Lara knew why that was so. With almost every interaction she had with the Holy Spirit, there was always much more to the conversation than the topic at hand. It was her job to study and apply herself and find out what he was trying to tell her. She was being tested.

"This way," she directed. Oppenheimer was only too ready to be led. He clearly needed a mental break. Lara felt a tug on her person, from the inside. She was being pushed in the direction of an obscure door. It did not seem like a doorway that was often used. It was unmarked and solid. She looked down the hallway; in both directions there was no one in sight. She turned the doorknob and ushered the professor through the door. She closed the door behind them.

They were surrounded by white light. It was a quiet and unfamiliar place. They should have been surprised;

this place did not seem like a room. It was more like a landscape. They could almost hear a trickle of water nearby—was it a creek?

Lara knew she might not have much time with the professor. Although he was in a somewhat vulnerable state of mind, she also sensed that he had an open mind. Maybe the scene around them made that possible.

"Professor, I am from the future. My name is Lara Tigler. For some reason, God transports me through time sometimes. Most of the trips are made to help correct some small problem. I do not know much more than that. But it really does seem that God is actively working to make the crooked places straight. And he does not always use conventional timelines to do it!" She was excited. Clearly this man had the intellectual capacity needed to understand all that she was saying, if not also the belief.

She went on, "Back in the 1950s, you were in a limousine with two military members, and you had a secretary taking notes. You put some of the notes into your Bible. I know because I was the secretary."

His eyes opened wide. But he said nothing. She went on.

"Is there something I need to know? Can I help you? I know about the alien-human conspiracy to nudge people into making decisions that they may not want to make. Just give me a clue. I can help solve this mystery. Maybe I can stop it from happening. You seemed to indicate, when we were in the limousine, that this catastrophic manipulation of the human mind was likely to occur sometime in the future. We do have nanotechnology now. We have the capacity to interface artificial intelligence directly with the human brain, even in my time. Granted, the technology is in its infancy."

Oppenheimer was stunned, but he was taking it all in and calculating what he could do to help. "The key is the human element of the plot. I have never had the privilege to communicate with the aliens involved."

Lara could not help thinking that Oppenheimer was leaving the possibility open to the fact that he had had contact with other alien species. But she knew, and he probably did too, that they had better stick to the current subject. They did not know how much time they had together in this strange place.

"There is a large, underground complex in Virginia. The contractor responsible for making robotic technology had a hidden access made to the facility. It was such high clearance, and access was so limited, that it is likely that that port of entry still exists, even in your time." Lara was stunned. Robotic? She realized that she had no idea when robots were first researched in the United States. And even if she looked that up, chances were the date given would be incorrect. Looks like the military was on top of robotic research decades before it was popularly understood to have begun.

"How do I find this access point?" Lara wanted to know. It looked like she would be making a trip out to Virginia to visit her in-laws.

"The contractor gave the land to a museum. I think it is called something like 'Futuristic Military Weapons.'" Some museum, Lara thought. "Maybe it still exists in your time?" The professor was warming up to the subject now. He seemed happier, his face relaxed.

"Do you know what kind of facility was underground?" Lara knew that the underground facility was the key to solving this mystery, this future crime on humanity. At least she hoped the appropriate word here was *future*. If the alien-human conspiracy had already started its attempt to trick the human race, then she did not have much time. Better to prevent disaster than to clean up a cosmic mess after the fact. Even if she somehow found this underground facility, she had no idea how she was going to penetrate its defenses. But one thing at a time. She waited for the professor's answer.

"It was a lab. There was a lot of research going on. Scientists were interested in finding a physical basis for describing and experimenting with heaven and hell. Whether or not humans believed in such things was somewhat unimportant, if these places really did exist. If they could experiment successfully, then they knew, with time, they could manipulate others successfully. It was just a matter of time." He spoke soberly. Lara knew that time was of the essence. It was all about time.

CHAPTER FIFTEEN

THE ALIEN

Lara and the twins went to bed right after dinner. The boys were exhausted. For them, it had been a remarkable weekend, to say the least. They had visited a beach literally worlds away from their own. Daddy was still gone on yet another deployment. And they had just returned from a weeklong camping trip with their grandparents and had had to tell them goodbye at the airport. They were done for the night.

As for Lara, she had to process an assassination attempt on her person, an escape, multiple time- and space-travel excursions, and meeting both her husband and Oppenheimer, only to be torn away from them. What gave her solace was knowing that her husband was all right. Also Oppenheimer seemed to have reached some sort of resignation about his part in developing the atomic bomb. And, Lara hoped, her visit with him might have served a good purpose in letting him know that he was not alone.

That brought Lara's thoughts right back to where they belonged, God. Ultimately, it was God who made almost all of her connections and progress possible. As much as she wished he was a bit more verbal sometimes, he/she really did come through for her. And his hands-off approach did keep her independent wheels spinning. She needed to be on the alert and not give in to a dependent mindset. So, all in all, she was pretty happy with his approach, even if it was maddeningly sparse sometimes.

All those years she had always wondered, why her? Why was she chosen to go back in time and correct those little might-have-beens? Was it all preparation for her current assignment? She knew God was in control. He was just letting time play itself out, so that she would eventually learn how to fall in line. How to express love. How to give. How to help others.

The scale of the current mystery did not bother Lara. Years ago, if she was given an alien-human conspiracy mystery to solve, she might have cried foul. But she guessed God's preparation had been just right. He knew what it would take for her to be ready, and she was.

Aravia's planet came to mind. The stadium and all of its varied audience members were out of this world, literally. She laughed out loud remembering Jesus's comic routine. What an introduction! And yet it was more than that. It was a reminder. No matter what happens, do not let yourself get too bogged down. Remember that God never gives us more than we can handle! And at the same time, it is our responsibility to do our best with what has been given. No good deed goes unpunished, as the saying goes.

She calmed her mind even more. The laughter turned to joy. The joy turned to peace. She looked deeper inside her mind and soul. It was quiet, hopeful. She saw a lake and then a shore. Sitting on the shore was a woman; Lara recognized her from the stadium. She was wearing traditional Asian-Indian clothes. She spoke only one word, "Virginia."

Virginia? Lara knew what the woman was trying to say: even though tomorrow was a workday, she had to make traveling to Virginia a priority. It was Thanksgiving next month. Tomorrow she would ask her in-laws (and her husband) if the family could spend the holiday with them. Now all Lara had to do was fall into a restful and restorative sleep. Tomorrow was another day, and she had better be ready.

Lara thanked the lady and prayed to God, thanking him/her for all that she was and all that she had been given. She prayed for her husband and children's safety and then she fell asleep, her dog in between her legs and her favorite pillow under her head.

She woke up and it was Monday morning. The usual busy routine began, but she knew that she had to make it a priority to start making travel arrangements to visit Virginia. She put in a call to her husband. He did not answer, but she made sure to ask if the family could go to visit the grandparents back east for the holiday. That done, Lara got ready for the day. When the nanny arrived, bright and early at 6:00 a.m., Lara took the dog for a much-needed walk.

Instead of the dog park or the usual two-mile walk that she might do in the evenings or early in the morning on the weekends, Lara took her dog to the small grassy area near the end of her block. It was not a dog park per se, and she could not let the dog off the leash, but at least it was a chance to meet and greet other dogs and roll on the grass. She saw a man at the other end of the park. He was alone, which was unusual. It was usually just joggers and dog walkers this early in the morning. Lara kept a watchful eye, but still made her way around the small area.

As she approached, the man settled in and sat on the nearby bench. Not a threatening posture, but still Lara was wary.

"We know you have been contacted," he said, giving the impression that he did not know much.

"Good morning. Contacted? Do you mean by the HOA? Anything going on in our community I need to know about?" Lara was not sure what exactly this man was talking about. But just in case he was up to no good, she thought she might stall a bit.

"We do not have much sympathy or tolerance for you mystic travelers. We don't like interference. It's not too late for you to just walk away." This time his sitting posture did not seem casual, but preparatory. Lara did not doubt that this man had a quick get-up-and-go time.

Lara mused, "Ahh. I see. You're not from here, are you?" She knew that he was an alien. And she also knew that he was fishing, he was guessing. "I should probably warn you that I carry protection. And believe me, I know what I am doing."

Although he did not show any outward signs of fear, Lara knew that the dog and the gun she carried were in no way small deterrents. It was broad daylight, and even though there were few people up this early in the morning, it was only a matter of time until the next jogger or dog walker came strolling by.

Lara did not want to linger; if this man was so near her home, then she must get back to the house and make sure that the nanny and twins were not accosted in any way. "Catch you later," Lara offered. She did not mean it as a threat, but if he took it that way, then that was fine with her. She told her dog to heel in a firm and authoritative voice and turned her back on this menacing stranger. She hurried home.

CHAPTER SIXTEEN

CONSPIRACY

All was well at home. It was time to get to work and start a productive day. Lara kissed her boys goodbye and drove off.

Work was pleasant and busy, just how she liked it. She was old enough now, and had been practicing medicine for a few decades, so her level of efficiency was through the roof. Because her patients were all established, she knew them like the back of her hand. It was second nature to accurately diagnosis and treat her patients. All her recent paranormal and supernatural experiences were remarkable, but her focus on her patients precluded any unwanted intrusion into her clinical acumen process. It was only when she reached her lunch break that she took a moment to check her personal messages for any reply from her husband.

To Lara's delight, her husband had replied. He may have been thousands of miles from home, but she could count on him to think of her needs and be prompt. He was only too happy to agree to spending the Thanksgiving holiday with his parents. That approval obtained, Lara's next task was to contact her mother-in-law.

"Hello, Grandma Bear," Lara said as soon as her mother-in-law answered the phone. "How are you doing today?"

"Oh, Lara, how pleasant to hear from you. It feels like yesterday when I saw you last." Her mother-in-law had a fantastic sense of humor. She was capable of making a joke on nearly every level, but it was the sophisticated jokes that gave Lara the best giggles.

"That's right. It really does." Although Lara could not tell her mother-in-law that time was certainly not passing normally since she had last seen her, it did not necessarily feel like yesterday since Lara had seen her; she had visited her son and a professor from the past, all in the short time frame since she had last seen her mother-in-law. "So I was talking with Adam. He says we can visit you for Thanksgiving this year. Would that work with your schedule?"

Lara loved her mother-in-law. Even though Lara might call her months in advance, her mother-in-law seemed to relish making arrangements for the holidays. And of course seeing her grandchildren was always top priority. Lara never felt like she was intruding; it always felt like her in-laws were eager to see her and the boys.

"Yes, that would be wonderful! I am not sure that everyone can be there, but yes, me and Papa will definitely host you for the holiday!" Just like Lara's mom, Grandma Bear was always eager to have all of the extended family included if possible. Lara had to admit, she was looking forward to seeing her infant niece. It was an added bonus visiting Virginia, being able to see extended family, since all of Adam's immediate family lived in the Virginia area.

That task completed, Lara's next message was from Netflix. The producer had forwarded a list of potential agents who were familiar with streaming productions and what authors might need in a contract. Lara replied with a thank you and made a mental note to look over the agent list later in the evening.

The other messages were business as usual. Lara quickly emptied all of her personal and work to-do lists. Then it was back to the grindstone, seeing patients late into the afternoon and early evening.

When Lara got home, she was eager to see her children and the nanny. The reports from school were all good for the day. Lara could kick back and just spend quality time with her adorable twins. The boys played outside in their somewhat private cul-de-sac. A few neighborhood kids joined in. It was a nice chance to chat with her two neighbors on either side. More than once, Lara reflected how grateful she was to have good neighbors. Making small talk and spending time outside was one of life's little pleasures.

Emily, the mom on the right-hand side of Lara's house, brought up something unusual.

"I noticed a white van parked in front of your house, Lara. It did not have any markings so I cannot say it was a utility or something like that. When I checked back in a few hours, it was still there. I have no idea who that was." It was a mystery to Lara too. But she knew that her house had excellent security. No breach in security had been detected.

"I don't know either, but thanks for telling me." Lara was hoping that her hidden security cameras might pick up some information on the strange vehicle. She would ask Hubby to review the security camera footage. Quickly Lara texted her husband; she used a predetermined code, known only to them, asking Hubby to do just that. He would get back to her soon, Lara was certain.

More than once, Lara was glad for their heightened security measures. Between the nanny and the tight security at her children's school, she had little concern that her children would be in danger. Still, Lara wanted to give the nanny a heads-up to be extra vigilant. She used the white van as an excuse to inform the nanny to be cautious, even more than usual. The nanny did not need any more reason than that. She gave a special nod of understanding and readily agreed to be on the lookout.

Lara's neighbor on the left could not help but chime in, "Crime is on the rise, violent crime. We all need to be ready to defend ourselves. I've never seen so many Americans who seem to be enraged. They're out of their minds!"

Lara knew that the public went through phases over long periods of time. Currently, extremist violence was nearly all from the right end of the political spectrum. But in the past, there had been similar disruptive acts of violence that came from the left. She was thinking of the Puerto Rican Nationalists, the Weather Underground, and nearly a dozen other groups. During the 1970s protest bombings by these fringe groups were commonplace. The difference then compared to now was that the general population was not approving of these bombings. But nowadays, it seemed that millions upon millions of ordinary citizens on the right were almost openly supportive of violent acts, even seditious acts, against the government. Lara could not help thinking about her father-in-law.

Papa was a great man in Lara's opinion. And a great Christian. She wondered how Papa could reconcile voting for Trump, an obviously silly and bad man, to the highest office in the land in 2016 and 2020. Papa was an independent politically, and he was a man of incredibly good sense. It just did not add up.

And even more distressing, it was only recently, when she and Papa had been at the gym together, that Papa confided in Lara (and really, Lara got the sense that he was trying to persuade her to the "right" view) that he sympathized with the insurrectionists at the capitol on January 6, 2021. He went on to blame the insurrection on Maxine Waters, a Black woman and congressional representative from California.

It was laughable, but her father-in-law was not laughing! Lara wondered, could the human-alien nudge conspiracy have already begun? She knew Fox News, among other right-wing news outlets, had brazenly participated in antigovernment propaganda. Ironically, Fox News was operating almost as a state media during the Trump presidency, echoing and directing Trump's every move.

Up until 2019, Rupert Murdoch owned Fox News,and after the sale to Disney, he then became their chairperson. He wielded incredible power over right-wing media outlets that spun off the main Fox News corporation.. Could one man, or both men, be responsible for so many ordinary citizens not using their common sense? How could so many people, including her father-in-law, be duped into supporting one of the worst human beings on the planet, i.e., Donald Trump? How could they believe that destroying our democracy was a *good thing*?

Lara checked with her inner knowing. She could not sense a hidden technology in the messaging from the right. It really did seem that Rupert Murdoch, or perhaps a few others on the right, were strong influencers in the corrupt right-wing narrative. But Lara wondered, could these same men have been victimized somehow? Could powerful men on the right have served as guinea pigs for the human-alien conspiracy? If so, the test launch of the human-alien conspiracy certainly seemed to have been a resounding success.

Lara moved with fresh urgency. She now had a better idea about what she was up against. It was looking more and more like her country was turning into a bad timeline from a *Back to the Future* movie. Somehow or other, these few very bad and very powerful men had gained undue influence over the general population. And Lara had to be the one to set the timeline back to its proper direction. She knew that she could not undo what had already occurred. But if she could somehow oust the bad guys who were really behind this violent chaos afflicting America, then the timeline could naturally fall back into its proper consonance.

Only time would tell, but Lara had to work fast.

"Okay, boys, it's time for bed. Tomorrow is another day," she called out while they were playing.

It was a school night, so the twins knew the established routine. Reluctantly but obediently, they ran indoors, saying goodbye to their friends along the way.

After their baths, the boys went to bed. And Lara went to bed too; she was eager to sleep and dream. Never had the phrase "sleep on it" held more meaning. Lara knew that adventures lay ahead. But she also knew that she might be in for some mortal danger. She had to be prepared for whatever may come her way.

CHAPTER SEVENTEEN

THE BAHAMA CONNECTION

Lara awoke with a start. She knew, somehow, that she had overslept a bit. She never used an alarm clock. She just naturally woke up at her desired time. But today was different. This human-alien conspiracy was hitting too close to home. Not only did she have to worry about her own safety but her children's safety as well. The stakes were getting higher. The bad actors were moving in. Time was running out.

She realized that she had forgotten to review the list of agents who might represent her interest in dealing with Netflix. She would have to look at that during her lunch break or after work. There was no time now. Once she was ready, she walked the dog and said her goodbyes to her children and the nanny. Nothing untoward occurred. She could breathe a sigh of relief.

The day passed without incident. When she got home, she found that the twins also had an unremarkable day. She was relieved. Maybe the pace of events might slow down for a bit.

She could not find a message from her husband. But Lara was sure that he would get back to her about the van as soon as he could. She was not in the mood, nor did she have the time, to peruse hours of video surveillance tape. The boys were quietly doing homework. Lara took this quiet moment to engage in some much-needed prayer. She centered her mind and spirit on communication with God.

"Our Father and Mother who art in heaven..." she chanted. She always included Mother God in the Lord's Prayer. It was twenty years into being a Christian when she finally found out that there is a mother aspect to God. She gave the prayer nearly her complete attention. It made her feel calm and not as fearful as before.

She turned to the list of agents. She spent considerable time reading about each agent and looking up their customer reviews online. One agent caught her eye; his office address was listed in the Bahamas. Lara had just returned from there; her medical conference had been on the same island. Why that island would be important Lara had no idea. But if perchance she had to visit the agent at his main office in the Caribbean, then she could use that opportunity to investigate the assassin, assuming the trail had not gone cold. It was a long shot, but Lara was game.

Her best guess was that the assassin was sent by the human element of the conspiracy. And she was pretty sure that the man on the bench was part of the alien component. She wondered how much the two partners cooperated and planned together. Was it possible that one hand did not know what the other hand was doing? Perhaps the two conspirators did not trust each other that much. Lara was counting on that.

Isaiah was looking over Mommy's shoulder. "Mommy, I love that beach, can we go?"

Lara's laptop still held an image from her Caribbean search. There was a beautiful blue sky and a white-sand beach. There was nothing otherworldly about it, and it sure looked tempting. "Yes, why not? Good idea. I'll ask Daddy about it next time I talk with him."

Isaiah was pleased. "Let's phone Daddy now." Let's, thought Lara. She called his number, and he answered after a few rings. He sounded haggard.

"Nothing," he said enigmatically. But Lara knew that he did not want to explain his vehicle search in front of the boys. The van was not traceable.

"Okay." Lara was disappointed but not surprised. "Hey, babe, will you be back in time for Thanksgiving? After Virginia, we can all take a week off and go to that same island where my conference was." He knew that it was no coincidence that Lara wanted to go back. He had daydreamed more than a few times about killing that assassin. He wanted to solve this mystery just as much as Lara did. But she would have to explain the coincidence of the agent's office address being on the same island another time.

Adam explained that he would be back in time; that is why he was so tired. He and his squadron were doing extra shifts, nearly round the clock, trying to wrap up their mission. As he and the twins started talking with each other on the phone, Lara took the time to message her Netflix contact. She let them know her agent of choice, and they replied that they would put her in touch with them as soon as possible. That done, Lara put all her attention on the family call. It was time to play hide-and-seek, and this time there was no danger. Just fun, the way it should be.

CHAPTER EIGHTEEN

THE LOGO

It felt like weeks until Lara heard back from Candy Trix, her Netflix contact. Work was going well; the kids were doing well at school. Lara was getting antsy for her husband to return home from his deployment. Time had passed.

No new insights or time-travel experiences had occurred. Lara was not averse to more adventures; she honestly thought that the mystery was biding its time. Timing was everything, and she did not know how to force it or even have the desire to do so. The next big clue that she was looking for was in Virginia. She wanted to find that old museum that Professor Oppenheimer had told her about. Future weapons? She wondered what those could be.

In spare moments she read a biography about the professor. It was not brutally honest; it was more academic and superficial. She still had questions about the man. She wanted to know more. What brought him to study science in the first place? Did he find that science was sufficiently meaningful after helping to invent the world's first atomic bomb? How much did he know about the human-alien conspiracy? And was he complicit?

She knew enough about solving mysteries to let these questions simply present themselves to her mind. She must not push too much or let her own biases take over the narrative. She had to remain open.

The phone rang. It was Candy. "Hello, Dr. Tigler."

Lara hadn't even spoken yet; Ms. Trix took charge of the conversation well before she confirmed it was a two-way communication. Lara was fine with that. Let the process unfold. Wait and listen.

"Hello there," Lara replied. "How are you?"

"Your agent wants to meet in person. He only gave two options, here, in California, or at his office, in the Bahamas." She got right down to the purpose of the call.

Lara thought fast, but she knew that the only good option was the Caribbean. But why would anyone want to travel so far? She did not want to tip Candy off that she had an ulterior motive. "Our family is planning to visit my in-laws for the Thanksgiving weekend; they live in Virginia. I suppose traveling to the Bahamas would be easier from the Eastern Seaboard. Kansas does not have as many direct options to the Bahamas, or California for that matter. We could take a plane down to the island right after the long holiday weekend. Does that sound all right?"

Finally, Candy was warming up to the call. You could tell that she liked that the decision was easily made. She was the type of person that did not like to waste time.

"So glad to hear that the trip to see the agent is doable for you and your family. If we can help in any way to make your trip more comfortable, please do not hesitate to contact me. My office will be reimbursing you for the cost of your trip from Virginia to the Caribbean. No expense spared. So please feel free to purchase whatever type of flight you all need, food, the works. This includes your accommodations, for however long you and your family might need them." She went on to explain how the process worked, that the agent would be the one to spell everything out, that they would be in touch once all the paperwork was received on their end.

"Thank you, Ms. Trix," Lara said, but Candy immediately interjected.

"No thanks needed, Doc. And please, call me Candy. No formalities here. We're excited to work with you on this project. We know you are a busy practicing physician. We have done this type of thing many times, and I am sure that this process will go smoothly for all parties." She was sincere and eager to please. "We have all loved reading your book; we're excited to transform it into a hit series. Are you writing anything else?"

Lara was surprised that Candy was prolonging the call. She seemed to forget her briskness at the beginning of the conversation. "Yes, I am currently writing a science fiction novel about time travel. It's coming along much faster than my first book did. I have learned a lot about being an author." In her mind's eye, Lara could see Candy sitting in her office in California. She saw a young, beautiful woman. She was dressed in a sleek white blouse and a formfitting, but professional, gray-colored suit. Heels on her bare legs, flowing blond hair. Her cell phone was on her desk, not active, but Lara had the distinct impression that Candy had just put it down. Probably, she had been multitasking and the person she had been texting with had said goodbye. Candy was free to focus on just one task. What a concept for this up-and-coming producer.

"I can picture your office now, floor-to-ceiling windows, palm trees, and an ocean view. I hope to see it one day," Lara said with accuracy.

"If this is a test, then I pass. I know you can see me right now. Glad I came into the office today and did not choose to work from home." She started chuckling. Lara knew that the producer really did read her book. Clairvoyance was just one of the superpowers Lara had revealed in her first novel. Lara did not mean it as a test, but she was glad that this producer was sincere and honest, at least so far.

Lara chuckled herself. "You pass, Candy, but it's not really a test. If you could see me here in Kansas right now, you would be surprised to see snow on the ground. Winter begins in earnest in October in my neck of the woods."

"I see, well no wonder you chose the Caribbean. I am sending over an email right now; it has the introductory letter from your agent. Make sure to read it and all associated documents before you arrive on the island. Your agent is trustworthy but shrewd. You will have to be on your toes." Candy was signing off.

"Thanks for the heads-up. Have a great weekend," Lara said, then Candy gave her goodbye, which was just as warm, and hung up.

Lara opened her email. No time like the present, she thought. The logo at the top of the agent's letter surprised her. It was an American eagle with a fighter plane faded in the background, almost like a watermark. A military connection? How surprising. Yet how very not.

Adam was on his way home in a matter of days. Lara could not wait to show him this letter.

CHAPTER NINETEEN

F'IN' DANGEROUS

The big day was here. Adam was set to arrive at about noon. He planned to drive himself home from the air force base and decompress while the rest of the family finished their day at work and school. In military speak, this means he will pour himself a glass of whiskey and sit in the garage looking out at the sky. A lightning storm, or some other violent event of nature, being the perfect catharsis for his tormented wartime emotions.

Lara was beside herself with excitement. As always, she had difficulty sleeping the night before Adam's expected arrival. The pent-up energy and anticipation were worse with deployments, but TDYs (military business trips, essentially) caused the same nervous excitement. Being an old hand at frequent military deployments, she did not hesitate to take a 25 mg Benadryl last night. She did not want to waste her time; she knew the sleeplessness would be severe. As it was then, she slept like a baby and woke up feeling well rested.

She knew what her husband needed; he needed her! Adam would have an almost insatiable yearning to touch her. He needed Lara all to himself, no kids or dog running underfoot. But Lara was way ahead of her husband. She made sure to tell the nanny to keep the kids occupied at the library after school. Unbelievably, there was a karaoke event at the library today at 5:30 p.m. She always marveled at how much libraries have changed over the years. In her day, libraries were almost as silent as a tomb. But nowadays, there were the quiet sections of the library, and then there was so much more too. Why, people were expected to check out their own books on the computer! Like scanning your own groceries at the self-checkout lane. There were deluxe children's sections that sometimes rivaled the explorative displays at children's museums, and there were sophisticated homework centers.

When Lara got home, she just knew her husband was in the house. She could not see anything that had been moved, but she had a sixth sense when it came to her husband. If he was not downstairs, then he was upstairs in the toilet room. He ate quite a lot of food to feed his powerful muscles; going to the bathroom was a bigger event for him than it was for Lara.

As she walked into the master bedroom she saw them, flowers sitting prominently on the center of her dresser. With the mirror behind them, the flowers looked larger than life. The fresh scent in the room was powerful. Lara closed all the blinds; she began searching for romantic music on her smartphone. Marvin Gaye. It had to be Marvin Gaye's "Let's Get It On." As the music began to fill the room, Lara undressed completely and began to draw a bath in the twin's bathroom.

The cues were unmistakable. She knew her husband would follow suit. She loved when he was fresh shaven too. And who knows what the heck kind of grime was on his person from traveling for the past forty-eight hours. It was good to wash all our cares away. It was very good.

After some time, Lara saw her naked husband come into the bathroom; he approached her bathtub without saying a word. By the looks of him, he was already aroused, eager to talk with Lara using his body rather than his words. Lara shuddered with anticipation. She could feel the area below her pubic bone tingle with a gush of blood flow. Her stomach gurgled. Her husband smiled. He knew that whenever that happened, that meant that Lara's blood flow was shunting to her sexual organs. He grew larger with lust, anticipating a sensual entry.

He pulled on her nipples, hard. As he stepped into the bath, Lara reached for his scrotum. He saw the nail polish on her fingernails. He gave a nod of approval; his favorite color was the royal blue that she sometimes wore for parties and outings. To his satisfaction, Lara had let her fingernails grow a bit longer than the usual short, practical style that he was accustomed to. The sensation of getting scratched in his loins by his wife's glamorous fingernails was too much for him. He groaned with lust as he lifted Lara out of the tub, wet deadweight not being a deterrent to his urgent need.

Just as the couple arrived in the bedroom, they could hear Marvin Gaye singing about getting it on. They would answer that command; they would shout it on the mountaintops if they could. It was time. It was past time, and they had a lot of time to make up for.

Soon they were lost in a moment of connection, that undeniable experience of union where the two had become one. Groaning with waves of ecstasy, the constant pulsing, the sweat and harmony felt timeless. It was in that timeless moment when they both became aware that they were back in their honeymoon suite from many years ago. They were in Hawaii. Their present bodies had merged with their past bodies. It was like they were reliving the same moments from their actual honeymoon.

As surreal as this experience was, it certainly did not stop the momentum of their lovemaking; if anything, it enhanced it. Their combined rhythm seemed to hasten its beat. Just as they were both about to climax, they became aware of another aspect of the Pacific Ocean, not just the ocean that was in view just outside the window of their honeymoon suite. They realized that they were on a large ship in the Pacific Ocean, and they saw a huge explosion far away on the horizon. The combination of the danger of seeing the spread of the mushroom cloud coming directly toward them and the thrill of their simultaneous orgasm was overwhelming. They woke up out of their euphoria only to find that they were hot and sweating and lying safe in their bed back home in present-day Kansas.

They both sighed heavily. It was too much.

CHAPTER TWENTY

THE BENCH GUY

They lay there for what seemed like a long time, just looking up at the ceiling. Finally, Adam spoke, "What the heck happened?"

"I wish I knew," said Lara.

They lay there still, wondering what the mushroom cloud meant, wondering what it all meant. Try as she might, Lara had no intuition on the experience at all. Maybe this time it was Adam's turn to share an insight.

"What do you *feel* about the experience?" Lara always hesitated to use the word *feel* when talking to her husband. She knew that he was not keen to talk about his feelings. Most of the time, truth be told, he was not in touch with his feelings much at all.

Lara waited for what seemed like an eternity. Finally he spoke again, "I think I needed to experience this time-space travel for myself. I think it makes sense it happened during sex. Pretty much sex is all I think about."

She laughed. It may be that simple. God answers prayers, why shouldn't he answer Adam's? This time it was Lara who went along for the ride, and what a scary, yet thrilling, ride it was. More Adam's style than hers.

She recalled that nuclear testing was conducted in the Pacific Ocean between 1946 and 1962. It was highly possible that they had traveled through space and time to their honeymoon, and then they had traveled through space and time again to a nuclear test site somewhere in the mid-twentieth century.

They put on some music and talked at a low level, taking every precaution. Adam updated Lara on what he could about his deployment. Lara filled in some of the gaps on what the family had been experiencing lately. She wanted to talk about her father-in-law, but she felt that subject was too sensitive. She did not feel like opening a can of worms that might lead to nothing helpful. But she wondered what Adam thought about his dad. Did he fully understand his dad's point of view on authoritarianism? Did Adam share his dad's proclivity for cruelty and dominance?

Adam was a stern, sometimes harsh, man. But Lara had learned that that was the military training coming to the forefront. Lara knew Adam as a goofy, sweet person. At least when he was not feeling threatened and he was well fed and rested. Who has not seen that Snickers bar commercial where they depict a person with an angry affect until that person takes a bite of the candy bar and returns back to his normal self? Maybe that was all it was in Adam's case. But what about his father?

They heard the kids come into the house. They dressed hurriedly and ran downstairs.

What a hubbub it was when they all started hugging and talking at the same time. The nanny knew it was useless to try to communicate anything at all. With a nod Lara gave her leave, and the nanny left without being noticed. Adam would have to make it up to her another time. This moment was all for the family. And it was sweet.

The next morning was the beginning of a weekend. It was a no-brainer to go to the dog park and adjoining river. While Lara played with the dog, Adam took the boys to the deluxe monkey bar playground. As soon as she could, Lara joined them. It was sad to put the dog in the bed of the truck. But she really wanted to concentrate on playing with the family and it was lovely weather. Fresh air, with the windows open, and plenty of water was what the dog needed now.

Soon it became obvious that they all wanted to go to the forest area where the river was. Lara thought to bring the dog like she usually would, but she thought that the trip would be a quick one. They were all starving for an early lunch after all.

It was not long before they were traipsing through the bare branches of fall, getting stuck and caught amid ticks and poison ivy. They heard a crack. Everyone stopped. This area was usually deserted. No one in their right mind would hike through here. That was part of the reason they liked it; it was a sweet reward when they would reach the shallow, fresh water of the picturesque river. No one ever disturbed them here.

Adam gave the signal. Lara pulled out her concealed weapon. The twins pulled out their knives. Adam wielded his military-grade weapon, a knife that only he could carry, it was that heavy. Adam was thankful that he had taught his family to follow his lead. Lara was ready to obey his every word; she knew he had superior knowledge on survival and defense. Isaiah was scared, but he was eager to copy his father. Jacob was looking around; he seemed to be the one most keen on locating the stranger.

Everyone followed Jacob's gaze; it was off to the left. Adam signaled that he and Jacob would meet the stranger head on. Lara and Isaiah would circle around and try to confront the stranger from his rear. Maybe it was just a large animal, but they had better be ready, just in case.

Isaiah and Lara went off to the right, making as much noise as they could so as to cover Adam and Jacob. Maybe draw the stranger out or confuse him. Soon they were stepping in the clear water of the river, only ankle high. Lara heard the tiniest of sounds to her left. She signaled Isaiah to follow her stealthily. They crouched down and made their way to a bit of a clearing. Then they plowed through the branches fast, just as they heard Adam and Jacob rush in to where they thought the stranger was.

Lara shot her gun straight into the air and crouched down to the ground fast. She was trying to draw any gunfire that the stranger might use. Draw it away from Adam, so that they could have a fighting chance. And it worked.

Lara heard Adam tackling a man; she heard a painful groan, and she knew Adam was holding the stranger in an inescapable grip. She and Isaiah made their way to the men. To Lara's utter amazement, her husband was detaining the bench guy, the alien who had accosted her in the grassy park. Adam signaled the twins to help detain the stranger. They jumped onto the man and put all their weight down on his legs. It was not clear how long they could keep that up.

Lara pointed the gun directly at the bench guy. Her twins were able to move away to a safer distance. Adam nearly choked the man; he was thinking that he could kill him, and he would be fine with that.

"Don't," Lara spoke. It was all she had to say to help Adam come back to his senses. But he held his grip on the alien.

"Why are you attacking my family?" Adam demanded.

"I am impressed. I did not think you had it in you. All of you. I will have to rethink my approach next time," he said, almost with respect, and maybe even regret.

"Who are you? And why do you hate mystic travel-ers?" Lara wondered. After all, she did not know much about this man. She gave him the name of Bench Guy; that was how she would always remember him. But she could not know for sure what his involvement was with this current mystery. Maybe it was just a coincidence that he confronted her when he did. But she realized that it was menacing for him to accost her then, at the park, and it was menacing now.

"All in good time," he said sarcastically, and then he disappeared into thin air.

"Holy shit," said six-year-old Jacob.

Normally, all three of them would have pounced on Jacob and they would have told him to stop swear-ing, but all they could do was nod in agreement. It was obvious to Lara at least that Jacob had nailed the Bench Guy's character. The alien was the antithesis of a mystic traveler. Jacob had got it exactly right.

CHAPTER TWENTY-ONE

THANKSGIVING

The trip to Virginia was uneventful. It was like heaven staying in the old Tigler home. So nice to see Adam's side of the family's pictures displayed prominently on the stairway walls. Always a pleasure stepping back in time, whether in his parents' home or hers. The Thanksgiving dinner was all anyone could talk about and prepare for. It would be a while until Lara could escape to investigate the weapon museum. Adam was just as eager to do a little snooping around, but right now all he could think about was food and football.

Lara and Adam got to making the breakfast meal. They saw that the grandparents were already playing with the twins on the living room floor, doubtless some game that they had made up while camping only a couple months ago.

"I've been doing some research on that potential hidden lab Oppenheimer told you about. The NRA has a National Firearms Museum in Fairfax County. Maybe the hidden lab is under that museum? It is only a few hours from here. We can check it out, and on the way, we can visit my brother and our new niece in Richmond. Sound good?" Adam said hopefully.

"Sounds great," Lara said enthusiastically. It was not quite futuristic weapons kind of stuff, but it was as good a place to start as any other. Meanwhile, on the drive they could research more options, maybe find a lead. Plus the plan had an added bonus in that a trip to the NRA museum would not cause any raised eyebrows. Her parents-in-law already thought that she and Adam had an interest in collecting weapons. This trip seemed a bit far to go on a short holiday weekend, but they would probably be fine with watching the twins for a day.

Adam brought up the plan at the dining room table, where everybody was happily eating waffles with ice cream and sprinkles. Of course Lara and her health-conscious father-in-law chose fresh fruit and cream on their waffles, not that that was any less calorie laden. And the family certainly helped make all the fresh fruit disappear in record time. Well, today was going to be busy physically; they would need those calories! They would all visit the Virginia Living Museum in close-by Newport News, and then they would be playing in the backyard or at the nearby playground. Maybe the smart thing to do was eat light at dinnertime; that way tomorrow, Thanksgiving Day, they could be free to stuff themselves to their hearts' desire.

Papa loved the idea. He thought that Saturday was a good option for their trip to northern Virginia. Lara concurred. She really did want to do some shopping on Black Friday. Papa wondered if he could take the boys to a baseball camp event on both Friday and Saturday.

"That sounds perfect, Papa! Just perfect. What do you think, boys?" She and Adam had kept their plans open for the holiday week and boy was she glad that they had. She was sure the twins would say yes.

"Yes," they said in unison. That settled, there was nothing left to do but to enjoy good food and good company.

Thanksgiving Day went off without a hitch. Everybody pitched in to make sure that the afternoon meal was done to perfection. Every traditional dish was present, along with a few new recipes. Lara always enjoyed making her cranberry sauce from scratch. Adam made a delicious kale salad; of course, he had to add bacon to make sure it wasn't too modern for his taste. And Grandma decided to make her homemade bread with whole grain flour this year; it was delectable served warm with melting butter oozing into the fluffy bun.

Soon the topic of conversation turned to the baseball event and the museum trip. Papa was reminiscing about his father and how he had enjoyed playing baseball with him all those years ago. The twins listened with rapt attention.

"Can you tell us more about your father, Papa? What was he like?" Lara wanted to know more about her husband's side of the family. There was a long tradition of serving in the military, and Adam's grandfather was a contemporary of Oppenheimer's generation.

"He lived all over the world, of course. But he eventually settled in Florida. I know he worked in the Pacific for a time, because we lived in Hawaii when I was a boy." Everybody oohed and aahed at that.

"When was that?" Lara asked.

"It was 1958 to 1962, I think. Why?" Papa wondered.

"What was his main job at the time? Was he a pilot like Adam? Or an engineer, like you?" Lara did not want to press, but she really wondered if Adam's grandpa had any connection to nuclear testing.

"He was a pilot. But back in those days, you were not as fixed to one type of plane as you are now. He flew all sorts of aircraft. He even helped test new airplanes and models." Again, people at the table were impressed.

"I know there was nuclear testing in the Pacific around that time. Did he ever mention seeing an atomic bomb explode?" She held her breath.

"Why yes, I believe he did. Maybe that is why he died so young. He had an aggressive cancer at the end. I never put two and two together. He had so much exposure, all over the world. There is no way to know why he died so young, really." You could tell that Papa was sad just thinking about his father's premature death. Maybe that was why Papa lived life to the fullest and gave his grandchildren his all. He knew that life was fleeting, every moment should be cherished.

CHAPTER TWENTY-TWO

HER NEMESIS

Adam and Lara were driving on the highway to Fairfax County, Virginia. It was a crisp autumn day, blue skies and fresh air accompanying them on their journey. They were talking about their kids, giggling with pride at their presence of mind when dealing with the Bench Guy in the trees.

"And did you see how versatile Isaiah was? One moment he realized the danger, the next moment he was following orders like a good soldier, then he was like a hunter, secretly stalking his prey, quietly making his way through the thicket. He didn't like the noise of the bullet, but then who would? And he really came through for the family when he put all his weight on the Bench Guy's leg. Wow. I was so proud of the little dude." Lara was amazed at how well the boys accepted the intrusion in their hike and how well both of them had risen to the challenge to fight off danger.

Adam was smiling. "Yep. They are troopers, for sure. I was worried that they might have had bad dreams or something. Do you think their experience on Aravia's planet gave them some sort of spiritual lift? How can six-year-olds do so well in such extenuating circumstances?"

"I'm not sure. They pray with me every day. It is a matter of course for them to speak with God. And I guess we also give them strength and a firm foundation to stand on.

"It's weird, but I think they can already tell that the world does not quite understand the ways of God; it's like they know to tread lightly with unbelievers. And even with your parents, I am not concerned that they will spill the beans on their otherworldly experiences. They seem to know how to stick to the here and now, the importance of letting time run its course." There it was again, time.

All Lara and Adam could do was their best, to love their kids every day and to keep the faith. God was in control; there was no use overthinking. Anything.

"So true. God is in control," he agreed.

They pulled up to the museum. It seemed harmless enough. Lara surveyed the neighborhood. It was bustling and well kept. There were a lot of mature, well-grown trees. They were just changing their color; it was a charming scene.

"How about you go into the museum and check it out? I can walk around the grounds, look for any clues?" Lara said helpfully.

Adam knew that Lara was not an indoor person. If she had her way, she would walk with the dog everywhere, she liked being outside that much. And dogs that much. At the same time, he loved that her job was safe, indoors. It was true that Lara used a stand-up workstation; she went from exam room to exam room. Her physician work was not sedentary. But it was a secure, well-guarded facility. He knew the security staff personally. He could breathe easy, knowing that she and the kids were in good hands when he was away.

But Lara checking the outside perimeter, in a new place, did not exactly make him feel at ease. The family dog was not with them on this trip. They were not able to bring their firearms on the airplane, not exactly something they would push for when packing for the family.

"Be careful," he said.

Lara knew what she might be up against. She had gotten plenty of sleep the night before in preparation. Adam had done all the driving, so as not to raise her stress hormones one tiny bit. They both knew she might have to travel through time and space. Adam, too, was wondering what might lie in store for them. The tension in the car was palpable.

"Will do." They said a quick prayer and got out of the car. They kissed and went their separate ways, each with their cell phone well charged, the volume on the highest setting.

Lara found a walkway off to the right of the main building. There was a well-manicured garden adjacent to the path; clearly visitors were welcome. But she saw no other pedestrians. It was Saturday; you would think there would be others, but no matter. Maybe it was better this way, walking unseen.

She kept walking deeper into the large property. She was glad she wore her comfortable, neutral-appearing Skechers. Her casual skirt and layered tops were perfect for the outing; she looked stylish yet womanly, just the way she liked it. She didn't have to, but wearing her glasses had become a matter of course. She really only needed them for reading, and the prescription did help with her astigmatism. But she had found through the years that it was handy to keep them on just in case she had to do some quick reading on her phone, or even for texting cute, candid photos of the kids instantly to the grandparents.

Her instinct told her to silence her phone. Without hesitation, she did just that. She glanced around. She saw no one. Nothing on the path had changed. She saw a group of trees off to her left; quickly she moved into their protection. And not a moment too soon. Off in the distance, even further along the path, she heard voices. She could tell that there were at least two men in the group of people who were headed in her direction.

They were speaking in low tones; it was clear that they did not want to be overheard. "I don't see why we keep to the old ways. The password should be updated. I'm sick and tired of this game."

"We're up against something bigger than anything you can imagine. Time has passed, but the situation remains the same. You must be patient."

Lara mused. It could not be a coincidence that God wanted her to hear this conversation. Somehow she knew that the two men were talking about the "family name" that Oppenheimer had warned her about. In a flash, she realized that it was *her* family name. It was *Tigler*. Her husband's grandfather must have played some role in this mystery. Or maybe, somehow, someone involved knew that a mystic traveler would be on her way to save the day, with God's help. But how?

Bench Guy! It had to have been him.

She fumed with anger at the Bench Guy. After his failed attempt to kill her and her family, he had clearly upped his game. There was only one other person that she knew of that had the ability to travel through time at will, the devil. Maybe the devil couldn't travel through time per se, but he certainly had access to a lot of doors that led into different times.

She remembered seeing him in that peaceful, in-between place; she remembered his staunch opposition to letting her pass through that heavenly gate, the portal that had led to her husband. She just knew that the Bench Guy had made an alliance with Satan.

Lara thanked her lucky stars that she had kept her glasses on, and that her phone volumes were all on mute. She crouched down, even more hidden than before, and began texting her husband. She gave him the signal that she was delayed but safe. They used their predetermined secret code so that he understood that there were at least two men near Lara, and she was not able to slip away, not yet.

Adam was enjoying himself in the museum. Unlike Lara, there were no suspicious conversations to overhear. The museum was well lit and built for comfort. He moved from one informative display to the next. It was crowded and fun. His phone gave a loud alert notification. Quickly, he silenced it and saw Lara's message. His expression went from happy to enraged in an instant.

Determinedly, he left the museum. He wanted to confront these men. He wanted to neutralize any threat to his wife. He was on the war path.

Lara could hear the men pass her by, still walking toward the main garden, obviously headed toward the museum. But she dared not move from her hiding place; she knew to wait for her husband's signal. She had to remain where she was.

Far down the path, she heard a ruckus. Men were talking loudly, including her husband. She prayed that it would not come to blows. She knew that when men got to protecting anything, they could be laser focused and difficult to reason with. Her husband was protecting her, and the two men were protecting a vast human-alien conspiracy. She held her breath, praying.

Soon there was nothing but silence. She breathed with relief. Then she heard the voice she most wanted to hear in the world, "My love, you can come out now, it's safe."

She hugged Adam so hard. "What the heck happened back there? I thought you guys were going to kill each other."

"It was nothing. One of them bumped into me and I gave him a piece of my mind," he said proudly. Lara could tell he had been ready to kill them if they had given him the slightest provocation. The offending man must have sufficiently bowed down to her husband's indignance at being so rudely mistreated. He must have seen that Adam was ready for battle, and he must have backed down. Lucky for him.

CHAPTER TWENTY-THREE

THE SNAKE OIL SALESMAN

They were laughing and crying, all at the same time.
The Thanksgiving holiday had been a smashing success, but now it was time to part ways. Always
bittersweet to leave loved ones, but they all knew that
they would see each other again soon. Grandpa and
Grandma had walked with them as far as they could.
Now Adam and Lara and the twins had to enter the
security line; it was time.

Tearfully, they hugged one last time. "Have fun in
the Caribbean! Wish I was there with you." Papa would
have loved to come, but he just could not get away.
"Take pictures." Papa and Grandma waved them off,
hoping for the best and eager to see them again sometime soon.

The twins were loving this adventure. They had
thoroughly enjoyed the baseball camp, but now they
were looking forward to the picturesque beach that

Isaiah had seen on Mommy's computer. They couldn't believe their luck, a pool and a beach all at the same place; it was like heaven.

When they got to the hotel, they were impressed that that was where Mommy had been only a few months prior. Adam decided to take the boys directly to their room so that they could change for the pool. Lara wanted to speak with the concierge to thank him for his kindness in sending her things to her home in Kansas. She promised to join her family in the pool area as soon as she could.

Her conversation with the concierge was a pleasant one. Try as she might, though, she could not elicit any information on the assassin. He remembered Lara easily enough, but when it came to the assassin's description, it was like his mind was a blank, it did not ring any bells. She had thought the assassin was striking enough in her presentation that a man in his position, able to observe so much, would have remembered her. But clearly the concierge could not offer any leads.

As Lara was making her way toward the elevator bay, she saw a man accidentally bump into a lady. It was the assassin. As the lady bent down to collect the items that had flown out of her open purse, she looked directly at Lara's face. Lara held her breath; there was no way to evade her gaze. To Lara's astonishment, the assassin's face registered no recognition. She continued to complete her task and collect her items that had been strewn across the floor.

Something was fishy. Somehow Lara knew that this lady had never met her, not yet. But it was for sure the same person. Unless the assassin had an identical twin sister, this was the lady who had tried to kill Lara.

Time. It had to be something to do with time, and more specifically time travel. There it was again; her enemies were beginning to have access to time travel. But Lara was going to take advantage of this coincidence. She began helping the assassin lady pick up her things. She made small talk.

"Oh, thank you, I really appreciate it. I don't know what I was thinking, leaving my bag open like that. I won't be so careless again," said the assassin. And Lara knew that this lady was telling the truth. She would not want to leave any loose ends, not ever again.

As Lara was helping pick up the things on the floor, she noticed a piece of paper lying face down; thinking that this item, too, might belong to the assassin, she picked it up. Lara flipped it over and only had time to see the logo at the top of the letterhead; it was an eagle with a faint image of a fighter plane in the background, like a watermark design.

The assassin reached for the piece of paper and grabbed it, gratefully, "Thanks again, I sure do appreciate your kindness."

"Any time," Lara said, and the irony of the remark was not lost on her. The assassin walked away.

Lara rushed upstairs, eager to get changed and swim with her family. But she was even more eager to tell her husband that the assassin lady had been found! It was the right place, but apparently, the wrong time.

Adam could not believe it. It sounded impossible. But there it was, the impossible coming to life and in unexpected ways. Now he was unsure what to think. In the back of his mind, he had been ready to confront the assassin, but now things had changed. He wondered how this mystery would end, now he was worrying about it. If time was no longer linear, had the end already occurred? And could he and Lara somehow *skip* to the end?

It was decided that the entire family would go to the agent's office that next day. Adam could keep the boys busy in the waiting room or even accompany his wife in the meeting and the twins could simply watch their tablets. He wanted to keep the family together. He was beginning to realize that separating from one another, at any time, could lead to a greater separation in time and space than he was comfortable with. Since the twins were already involved, it would be better to stick together, at least for this meeting.

To Adam's delight, the agent's office was very accommodating. He did not get a sense of danger whatsoever, but still he was cautious. The agent sat at his oversize desk, clearly pontificating being his go-to demeanor. The twins were happily seated at a large conference table across the hall, playing games on their tablets. All the walls were glass, and the agent appeared to have no other clients in his office. They decided to leave the doors open so that the boys had easy access in case they needed anything. The administrative assistant, who was *not* the assassin lady but instead a pleasant, middle-aged, attractive woman practiced at entertaining clients, made sure to cater to the family's every need.

"I will gladly represent you, Dr. Tigler. I have been enjoying your work." As he fingered her hard copy book laying on his desk. "Netflix will probably make a smash hit from it. I have laid out the details of what I expect. But basically, I get 20 percent of all earnings. I've given you a list of attorneys. I highly encourage you to retain one. We want everything to be on the up-and-up, don't we?"

Somehow Lara knew that with this guy, nothing would be on the up-and-up, as he liked to phrase it, unless she made sure to watch every detail. Yes, hiring an attorney would be a prudent measure.

"Of course. Thank you, you come highly recommended," Lara said truthfully.

"Ahh. Yes. Candy Trix. Sweet girl. I look forward to meeting her again soon." Lara had no doubt that he did. The way that the agent was eyeing her, looking her up and down, made both Adam and Lara suspect that this man had few barriers in terms of behavior. He was probably thinking that he could have more than a business relationship with Candy. Or maybe to him, personal and business relationships were one and the same.

When they were safely back in their hotel room, Adam asked Lara, "What have we gotten ourselves into? This guy seems like he has a connection with the mystery. I trust him even less than I trust the Bench Guy."

"And that is saying a lot, I know," Lara said. But at least with the Bench Guy, she knew where she stood. With this agent things seemed murky, dirty.

But they had both agreed, no matter how slimy this agent was, they wanted to proceed with the agreement. Production would begin in Hollywood in a matter of weeks, not months, he had said. The agent had gone on and on explaining how they would meet all sorts of celebrities during production. He even boasted that media giants, such as Rupert Murdoch, might stop by the production studio. Apparently, the right-wing media business owner had an interest in branching out into streaming platforms such as Netflix.

Lara and Adam had been careful not to bat an eyelash when the agent had told them about Rupert Murdoch. They knew that they were on the right track, solving this mystery. They were just stunned to begin to see how all the pieces were fitting together. It was disconcerting to know that somehow, the agent was allied with the bad actor(s) responsible for the human-alien conspiracy.

And to know that this agent's partner or assistant, the assassin lady, would be sent into the past to kill Lara, well, it was not a pleasant prospect to say the least. The saying "what is done is done" did not seem to ring true anymore.

Lara had already lived through that experience. But seemingly, for the assassin lady, that experience was yet to come.

Lara and Adam were beginning to understand time. It was not a simple ladder that you climbed in one direction, either up or down. Time was more like a spiral staircase, or more like multiple spiral staircases next to one another. You could climb on the outside of the railing and jump down a level, or you could jump to the next staircase on the same level. There was more than one way to get around through time.

Or you could be like most people, and just go up the spiral staircase. Just go in one direction through time, never realizing that jumping levels or jumping from one staircase to the other was even a possibility.

What seemed impossible to most people, traveling through time, was not impossible at all really. The trick was to realize that time was a tool, and the people who knew how to use that tool masterfully had an advantage.

Maybe that was why God was setting Lara and Adam up for success in time. In the beginning of her life, Lara thought time was linear. Now she realized throughout her entire life, God was using her like a pawn. He had sent Lara on various time-travel adventures throughout her life. It was God who had told her to write her first book, after all. And now this book was giving her access to Hollywood, where apparently lived some bad actors (no pun intended). People who appeared to be involved in the human-alien nudge conspiracy, the time-travel mystery. The same mystery that God was helping her to solve.

God knew what would happen, through time, and he knew that he needed someone who knew the ins and outs of time. Slowly Lara and Adam were realizing just how complicated this time mystery was; they were realizing just how advantageous it was to see time as it really was rather than what they used to think it was.

They knew that time was always running out. Only eternity was timeless.

CHAPTER TWENTY-FOUR

INDIA

It was great to be back home in good old Kansas. The open sky and endless grasslands, while not as exotic as the Caribbean, still had their own special allure. The changing of the seasons was not subtle in the Midwest, especially in Kansas. There were no natural windbreaks across the Great Plains. The harshness of the storms and winds brought to mind the constant ebb and flow of strife in this life. Suffering, endurance, and especially tolerance were attributes that Kansans had in spades. Maybe that was why Lara just took for granted that she could handle this tremendous time mystery puzzle that God had laid in her lap. If he gave her a load, then she would bear it if she could. That was how it was in Kansas. You just dealt with it.

It was a lazy weekend. Adam and the boys were out in the front yard, playing in the snow. The dog was catching snowballs in the air, almost like the monkey in the middle game, only she caught the snowball much more frequently than kids catch the ball. Lara was looking out the front window, sipping her hot chocolate, savoring the coconut whipped cream and cinnamon on top.

Lara got to thinking about the time-travel mystery. She trusted God when he sent her back in time. She never once thought that her (slight) interference in those excursions was disruptive to the space-time continuum. But she began to wonder about the Bench Guy and his excursions through time and space. Was he causing any sort of damage to the universe? And how the heck was the assassin lady going to get sent back in time to attack her at the medical conference? The concierge had not recalled seeing the assassin lady. Maybe that was because she had not gone back in time yet, at least from his perspective.

Maybe a further disruption in the space-time continuum was preventable. Lara realized that California held her next big clue. She might run into the assassin lady on the production set. There might be a way to prevent malicious intent when it came to time travel, if that was even something that needed to be done. Or something that should be done.

Lara knew that lying was harmful to the fabric of the universe. Surely, traveling through time in order to cause harm was similarly disturbing to the cosmic plan. And that got Lara thinking about the human-alien nudge conspiracy. The bad actors at the military-industrial complex probably gained money and power from the conspiracy. But what did the aliens gain from it?

She looked out at the falling snow. Water. Water is the most consumed natural resource on planet earth. The second most consumed natural resource is concrete. Sand is needed for that. A certain type of sand, too. It has to be just right. That was why people were digging for sand at the bottom of rivers and not in the vast Sahara desert; it had to have a certain quality in order to be a good ingredient for concrete.

Lara knew that silica sand is used to make computer chips. Between concrete, the two heaviest utilizers of that natural resource being China, then India, and computer chips, it seemed that sand was of the utmost importance to the human race. Maybe sand was a resource that these aliens wanted as well. Lara remembered reading about the deadly world of India's sand-mining mafia. Between the United States military-industrial complex, which she knew was involved in the human-alien conspiracy, and the organized crime in India, Lara knew that the human race would be vulnerable on several fronts when it came to procuring its much-needed natural resources.

But this was all speculation. She needed real clues; she needed some insight into the alien perspective on all of this. That brought to mind the lady from India, the helpful fellow mystic traveler that she had met while on Aravia's planet. It was she who had confirmed that

Virginia was the next step in solving the human-alien conspiracy. Maybe Lara could connect with her again?

Lara calmed her mind. She quieted all hypothesizing. The natural flow of thinking was helpful, but thinking was only one tool; she knew that meditation and contemplation were equally as important. Gently, she rested her mug on the front windowsill. Adam's gaze fell on his wife; he just knew she was about to slip away into another time. He prayed so hard.

Lara found herself in a tropical and crowded place. She was wearing a traditional Indian dress, and there was the stench of pollution in the air. She was staring at fruit below her—she was in a marketplace—when she heard her name, "Lara, over here!"

Turning, she saw the same woman that had been in her vision about Virginia. "Sujita!" Lara called in reply. Somehow Lara knew this woman's name. It must have been that deep empathy they had experienced on Aravia's planet a few months ago. They knew each other. Even if their introduction was a bit unorthodox from an earthly standpoint, they had been effectively introduced.

"We must hurry, Lara." Sujita ushered Lara out of the general market area into a rather tiny passageway. They were moving quickly, passing countless onlookers as they scurried by.

"When are we?" Lara asked, now realizing that she might have traveled through time, not just space.

Sujita replied, "Aah, no time. I am not supposed to be away from my family. I am afraid they do not understand my new role as a mystic traveler." She knew that this was a gross understatement. Lara had an understanding that Sujita's family was very traditional. It would be unseemly for her to be walking around the village without a male chaperone.

Lara chuckled. She could see that Sujita had a wicked sense of humor. "Well, you helped me once. Is there anything I can do for you this time?" Lara said with equal irony.

"Yes, your Bench Guy has come to my hometown. He made reference to you when I last saw him." Lara had a questioning look. "Don't ask," Sujita said.

"Are we in any danger now?" Lara could see that they were in a tiny, dark room. But the din of people, although muffled here, was still audible. A bad guy could be hiding close by.

"I didn't let on that I knew you. I don't think the Bench Guy has any special insights, at least not like we do as mystic travelers. I think he is just guessing. But I do not know how he is getting his information. I was not able to intuit his name. But I do think you are correct; he is an alien. I think he is from our very own galaxy. I was able to see him in the heads of some of the others at the soccer stadium that day on Aravia's planet. But he may just be an agent or representative for an alien race that lives even farther away. It is unclear where his allegiance lies." She was out of breath. Clearly this type of clandestine meeting was new to her.

"Well, look no further then. I believe he is in cahoots with the devil," Lara said with certainty.

"I am Hindu. We do not believe in your devil. Are you sure?" It was obvious that Lara was stretching even Sujita's ability to be open minded.

"I don't know if he has another name, or role, in the Hindu religion. But I know for sure that he is what we Christians call the devil. I saw him in an almost heavenly, in-between place. There were a lot of doors and there was at least one gate. He seemed to have the ability to come and go at will. And he was definitely bad, not good. He seemed to have some access to time travel, and he seemed to want to prevent me from going through the doors and gate." Lara was trying to speak softly; she was worried about people, anyone, overhearing them.

"You have the ability to levitate, and I have the ability to make myself disappear." What? Lara was confused. The conversation had shifted. Lara began to wonder if her new friend was all there.

But soon Lara understood her friend's mysterious remark. Sujita could feel that their time with one another had ended a touch sooner than Lara could. Sujita was slipping away. "Sujita, don't go!" Lara begged. But it was too late. Lara, too, was slipping back into her own time and place; she was back home in Kansas.

"Sujita, I have a feeling we are not in India anymore," Lara said, mimicking Dorothy in *The Wizard of Oz*. But Lara's words were heard by no one; she was inside her house, standing at the front window, and she could see her family outside, still playing in the snow.

She began laughing anyway. That Kansas joke never gets old. And who doesn't like the movie *The Wizard of Oz*? Lara could tell that her drink was still hot; she saw steam coming up from the cup as the vapor met the cold air of the windowpane. She locked gazes with her husband. She knew he would understand completely why she was about to disappear from the window. Her next move was to the kitchen, where she would put a generous amount of Bailey's Irish Cream into her mug and drink it down with relief.

This was his cue to move everybody inside. The twins would get hot chocolates, too, and everybody would sit in front of the fireplace to get cozy, the dog too. And he would sip a strong whiskey and thank his lucky stars that his wife made it back from yet another mystical time journey. Little did he know that this time, her connection with God was not through a Christian lens, but through a pagan one. They both had a lot to learn about Hinduism and how it fit into the Creator's plan. But, even more interestingly, they would both learn about a new superpower that Lara apparently had, the ability to levitate. She did it regularly in her dreams; she wondered how she was going to put this new power into practice.

CHAPTER TWENTY-FIVE

THE EGOTISTICAL DEMON

It was good to be home. Really home. Although Lara wondered about her new friend in India. There was something pulling her from that part of the world; her connection with Sujita was undeniable. It was as though India played an important role in this time-travel mystery. Luckily Sujita was on the job. But it was clear that she needed Lara's help, and vice versa, Lara had already benefited from Sujita's help. For some reason, their respective knowledge about their religions was critical to understanding the roles that various actors were playing in this crime or conspiracy against humanity.

Lara recalled that the conspirators in the underground lab were interested in investigating and manipulating heaven and hell. She knew that these researchers were human; she understood that they were part of the powerful military-industrial complex. She knew that aliens played a role in this conspiracy, but she was getting more and more of an idea that the particular aliens involved were more in it for the money, so to speak. They were mercenaries. Maybe they wanted a steady supply of sand, maybe something else. The aliens must be supplying the researchers with something that they needed in return for access to some natural resource(s).

Prayer. Lara realized that her God responded to prayer. It was through prayer, chiefly, that her faith had been strengthened all these years. Faith that ultimately led to her salvation. In general, humans were less and less prayerful, at least in the Northern Hemisphere. Maybe the bad aliens were supplying the researchers with knowledge about how to communicate with the gods.

Lara knew that in many cultures all over the world, including in Mayan culture in what is present-day Mexico, in Indian culture, and in others, it was common practice to offer sacrifices to the gods. In the Judaic tradition, before Christ's arrival on the scene two thousand years ago, it was also common practice to offer God sacrifices.

Prayers and sacrifices. It was understood that the supernatural world almost fed on human prayers and sacrifices. It was as if human energies, their unconscious projections, are what shapes, almost creates, the divine. Could humans play a bigger role in creating the heavens, in creating heaven and hell, than just using their imagination to discern if heaven and hell even exist? Could they be part of the supernatural forces?

Could humans create a stronger heaven or a stronger hell? Through prayers and sacrifices? Lara let her mind wander to thoughts of Indian gods, what their devil and demon-like figures might be like. She did a general Google search. To her surprise, there was plenty of information on demons and divine entities in Indian mythology that were in opposition to the forces of goodness.

Lara quieted her mind. She calmed her spirit. As she looked inward, she noticed a lake. It had a smooth surface, it was placid. The area was vast, the flora most consistent with the Northern Canadian Rockies, pine trees and forest as far as the eye could see. It was late evening, but the light of dusk still made it possible to discern color and shapes in the distance.

About twenty feet out from shore, a statue-like figure began emerging from the lake's bottom. He was larger than human size but most reminiscent of a man, royalty. He was dressed in Indian garb, all red, with gold and jewels decorating almost every inch of clothing. He was holding a magnificent weapon like a huge, powerful sword. It was carefully protected in its sheath and held front and center of the man with its point facing downward.

"Are you a poet, lady of the evening?" the Indian lord asked.

Lara looked around. It was an odd question. She was alone on the shore. "Poet?" she said stupidly.

"Are you one that wrote the Vedas?" he questioned her patiently.

Now Lara was beginning to understand. In college, luckily, she had taken liberal arts courses; she had learned about the Vedas poems, written over three thousand years ago in India, in her comparative religions class. But as she was thinking this, she noticed that the man had a tusk on each side of his head. His face and eyes were distorted. He looked scary, but he was still patiently waiting for her reply.

"I guess I am, Lord," she said astutely, "I write long works of poem-like verse. I write adventures."

"You may write about my glory, my increasing fame and influence then. I have slept a long time, awaiting the praise and adoration of your kind. Finally, it has come again," he said with perfect calm. Apparently not realizing that she was a mystic traveler and not at all likely to glorify him.

"Is the Christian devil more powerful than you are?" she asked to bait him, to stall. She had to think fast. However this opportunity had been arranged, it was her chance to glean information. If she could only appeal to his vanity and self-absorption, to his ego, which was considerable.

His countenance was disturbed, but only slightly; he maintained his stoic expression when he said, "I am lord of my territory. I rule over those who are like me. Your Christian devil is elsewhere in time and space, but not far in character."

"Territory? Are you lord of India?" She did not know how to get him talking really. She just knew his costume looked like Sujita's culture. She was not entirely sure where and when he belonged.

There was the slightest hint at a smile on his lips. He was thinking of obtaining the elixir of immortality, the amrita in Sanskrit. He hungered for all the power and glory. But the slight upward tilt of his lips did not last. He immediately thought of all his many brothers, with whom he shared all of the Indian territory.

"Traitor!" It was the Bench Guy, to her left, running at her on the shore of the lake.

The lord of the depths was stunned at this interruption. He opened his eyes wider and saw the situation for what it was

a mystic traveler under the Creator's protection had somehow infiltrated his realm. But at the same time, he saw the Bench Guy, whom he immediately recognized as an ally, albeit a mortal one. The ground shook with his anger; the lake's water created a violent tsunami when he stomped his foot on the water's surface.

The great wave coming at them was all the distraction that Lara needed. As the Bench Guy looked at the wave with dread, she willed herself upward with all her might, not so much levitating, but flying. She focused all her spirit on the acceleration that she would need to reach the top of the wave and not succumb to its force. Ha! She made it. She had a feeling that the Bench Guy could have followed her, but maybe he did not have a friend like Sujita, a friend who could have given him a heads-up on the next skill needed in their game of cat and mouse.

She knew the Bench Guy was down in the strong currents of the water, but she was in the sky, practically face-to-face with the demon, an asura (demonic lord) of India. He scowled at her. With one swift motion, he swung his arm and jumped backward in order to slash her small body in half as the traitorous mystic traveler, in league with the daevas (good gods of India), deserved.

Lara saw a vision of Dorothy in *The Wizard of Oz*, thoughts of home always deep in her subconscious, and she clicked her heels together and pictured herself there. "There is no place like home," she began to say, to plead, and she rematerialized in her home just as she saw the sword about to lacerate her midriff.

CHAPTER TWENTY-SIX

VANQUISHING THE DEVIL

Sujita had been thrilled to meet her friend Lara in person. She, too, had been dismayed that their meeting had been cut short, she had thought by one of her gods. She and Lara had spent just enough time together to exchange much-needed information. They had not been given any more time than that.

It was all about time, and she and Lara were not exactly in control of it.

Like Lara, Sujita had been experiencing short time-travel excursions throughout her entire life. No one that she knew had similar experiences. Her parents were supportive and patient, but they were also devout Hindus. Although they believed in all the gods, it was hard to believe that their daughter was in nearly constant contact with them.

Unlike Lara, Sujita knew who was managing their time-travel excursions; it was none other than Narada, a lesser god who had the power to travel through time. Narada was gifted by Brahma, the Creator, with the boon of knowledge regarding the past, the present, and the future. He assisted the daevas (Indian gods of goodness) in combating evil. He had the power to travel to different worlds and realms, and apparently, he could send humans through time as well, because that is exactly what he had been doing for Sujita. And Lara.

Now Sujita wondered about her religion and Lara's. How could she and Lara be on the same team? Their worlds seemed so far apart, so different. Yet there it was. They were in the same stadium together on Aravia's planet, and that seemed right. And lately they had been in contact with one another via this strange, mystical connection that the gods had arranged.

Sujita wondered about Lara's time. She knew that Lara was an American, she knew Lara's *place* in this world. But what about her *time*? The way Lara talked, it almost seemed like she was from the future.

Sujita was happily living in the 1990s. Being a female and studying medicine, she did not exactly have it easy in India. Like China, and other places in the world, when a baby girl was born, it was not always a cause for celebration. As educated as much of the Indian population was, the cultural stigma of being a girl led to a relatively high rate of female infanticide. Even awareness programs warning against killing newborn baby girls were not effective in India, that is how much girls were looked down upon.

Sujita was thinking all this as she was riding her scooter to the medical campus. She was afforded some freedoms being a doctor in training. Her life was not as restricted as those of some of her female peers. She cherished the wind that tossed her thick braid, a welcome break from the tropical heat of the day; she was grateful that she was allowed to drive alone in the streets without a male chaperone. The large road was crowded with the chaos of vehicles going in all directions. There was no order in the streets. It was all honking and rushing.

She arrived early to campus. As she was parking her scooter, she spotted a fifty-year-old jamun tree in the nearby garden. She might sit under its welcome shade and consider eating its plentiful fruit. If she did eat it, then she knew that her lips would be stained from the juice of the fruit; it would take hours for that telltale mark to go away. Throwing all caution to the wind, she decided to toss her vanity aside and sit under the tree. She was so different from her classmates anyway, why not wear a symbol of that otherness? Nevertheless, she would be careful when she ate the berries, just in case.

Her mind moved back to her salvation experience just a few months ago. Sujita had been surprised to learn that Jesus Christ was real. She had had an inkling that Jesus was there with her when her soul had been saved. But so, too, was Krishna. Throughout her life, she had had plenty of mystical experiences with Krishna and many of the other Indian gods. She had little to no experience with the asuras (demons) of India, but she believed in their existence. She still believed in all the Indian gods; she was faithful.

Lara had said that the Christian devil was real. That was news to Sujita. It was an intellectual understanding only. It was still hard to take it all in, that the evil side of the divine was real, on the move, actively fomenting chaos and destruction. She shivered.

Now she realized that she really did know Jesus Christ, or at least, she was familiar with him. He had been overseeing her spiritual development all these years; she just did not realize that fact until she had reached the culmination of her faith. Only when she graduated, so to speak, only when she was saved, did she come to understand Jesus's presence in her life. It was a good feeling, being hugged by a God she hardly knew.

She knew enough about Christian mythology to recall that Jesus had defeated the devil. It was confusing why and how the devil was still able to roam the world and cause strife. She was beginning to understand that the divine was even more complicated than she had thought, and that was saying a lot coming from a pagan!

She was pensive. She knew that Jesus Christ and Krishna's lives had many parallels. They were both reincarnations of a triune God. But it was Sujita's understanding that the Christian God was not really made up of three separate entities like her gods; they were three different aspects of the one Christian God. Maybe a nuanced difference, but a critical one. Hers was a religion of many gods, and Lara's was a religion of the one true God.

Both Jesus and Krishna had been tempted by demons or demon-like entities. They had both worked miracles and been transfigured. They had both predicted their own deaths. She now realized that her religion was even more true, even more alive, than she had ever imagined. And unbelievably, so was Lara's.

"Sujita? It's time we had another talk." It was the Bench Guy. He had walked right up to Sujita; she was that deep in thought.

"I know that you are a liar and a thief! And you tried to kill my friend." Sujita was losing it a bit; his unexpected intrusion on her little haven was throwing her off.

"So you do know Lara. I knew it." He was speaking as much to himself as he was to her.

Sujita kicked herself mentally. How could she have let that slip? She had revealed her relationship with Lara. She hoped that this knowledge did not somehow disadvantage Lara in the future.

Future? She did not know when and where he and Lara might meet again. But she hoped and prayed that Lara would prevail if they did. Maybe she could warn Lara somehow? She had to throw the Bench Guy off, put him on the defense, buy some time.

"Why are you helping the mafia? You know they wreak havoc in this neighborhood." She knew that the Bench Guy did not care about her community. But she wanted to get him thinking about something else.

"It's not just me, Sujita; one of your brothers is helping me. It was he that told me about your little adventures in time." Sujita was stunned into silence. Many years ago, Sujita had confided in her brother Pavan about her time-travel adventures. They were close in age, and in their childhood, they had been the best of friends. But somewhere along the line, he had gotten in with the wrong crowd at school. He had become more and more distant. Sujita was sure he was abusing alcohol, maybe even gambling.

It cut like a knife to find out that her estranged brother had betrayed her, and to the Bench Guy of all people. Pavan just had no idea how far his treachery was reaching. He was selfish and lacked any imagination. He was lost. It was like he flew away from the safety and love of the family home, never to return. And no wonder, his name literally meant wind; he was named after the god of wind, Pavan.

The Bench Guy reached for Sujita's elbow; she knew she should get away. As she wrenched her left arm away from his grip, she willed herself to disappear, but he held on like a vice. As she was disappearing, she found herself traveling through time and space, and she knew that the Bench Guy was coming along for the ride.

They both found themselves lying on the ground, in that in-between place, the whitish space where Lara had found the gate that had led to her husband while he had been deployed in Europe. The devil was standing nearby, not surprised to see the Bench Guy, but very much surprised, and pleased, to see Sujita.

"We meet at last, faithful one. How fitting to meet you here." The devil knew Sujita. He had wanted to torment her for the longest time, but she had kept him at bay because she was always so pure, so faithful. Now his servant the Bench Guy had inadvertently brought her here; he had brought her to the lion's den. The devil felt his mouth salivate; he was anticipating a cruel scene.

"I see it all now. You're the broker," she said to the Bench Guy. She now knew that he was the one managing the exchange between the aliens and the military-industrial complex and probably also the Indian mafia in her neighborhood.

The Bench Guy looked at her blankly. He had been all bravado before, but clearly the devil took the life out of him. He was as much a prisoner as Sujita was, but he was too dumb to see it that way.

Sujita was out of her league. Unlike Lara, she had no preparation for this meeting. She had lived a relatively sheltered life. She was a young woman to Lara's more mature years. She knew that there would be no one to come save her here; there was nowhere to run to, there was nowhere to hide.

She glanced around, and she saw countless doors. But they were all well spaced out and she knew that making a sprint for one of those doors would be hopeless.

If fighting was futile, then she had no other option but to turn to her faith. If this was the end, then so be it. She would just let evil be. She would not fight it. She would surrender. But the only surrender she was capable of was a pure one.

Without thinking she said, "Jesus is the Lord and Savior of the world." She could not tell you in that instance why she even said those exact words. But she knew that those were the words, the only words, that made sense. It was what the devil needed to hear, and anyway, she knew them to be the truth.

The devil's jaw dropped. He was transfixed with horror and dread. She had said the only words that had the power to banish him from this place.

Immediately they were all aware of a great wind, like an explosion, and all the doors blew open. It was like an airplane was flying at thirty-five thousand feet, and all of a sudden a door had opened, sucking everything out into the sky.

It was like all the air was being sucked out the open doorways. Sujita saw the devil turn into black ashes, and his dust blew away, his ashes blowing out the doors. The last expression on his face was an angry one. He vowed to get even with Sujita for banishing him from this place of access and dominion.

But soon she had something else to think about. Both she and the Bench Guy were blown up into the air, twirling around uncontrollably. She saw the Bench

Guy get sucked out one of the doors and then everything stopped.

She never fell to the ground. Instead all the doors and all the whiteness just disappeared. She was alone, floating in nothingness.

Sujita heard a beautiful, deep voice say, "Well done dear one, well done." It was Father-Mother God. She knew instinctively that this was the Creator of the entire cosmos. He/she was above and beyond her gods. This was the one true God that Lara worshipped.

"Father-Mother?" she said, not knowing what to say.

"I am," he/she said simply.

"What happened to everything?" Sujita said with good reason; the universe did not seem to exist.

"You have transcended time and place. You are," he/she said patiently.

Sujita had never felt more alive. Finally, all context had been removed, just like she had intuitively known could happen, and she was exactly who she was supposed to be. She could not be labeled as a she. She was not a doctor. She was not not a doctor. She was not Indian. She just was. She existed.

"Do I have to go back? I never really belonged," she said with great hope. As much as she loved being a mystic traveler, even that job seemed too limiting for her. She always had an idea that there was something more.

"No. You may change your destiny if you wish." She was elated.

"What does that mean? Am I to join you?" She was amazed. How could this be?

"Yes, you can join us and remain," he/she said kindly.

Sujita was about to leap into God's arms and never turn back, but she remembered that other life she used to live. And she remembered that strange occupation that she used to have as a mystic traveler. "May I say goodbye to my family? To Lara?" She held only a slight recollection of that old life now, but she still knew that there must be some closure, if not for her, then for them.

"Of course, no time like the present," God said. Sujita laughed. It was going to be a long eternity.

CHAPTER TWENTY-SEVEN

GOODBYE

The Christmas and New Year's holidays had come
and gone. It had all been one big, happy blur. Lara
and her family were hitting their stride by mid-January,
and school and work were all going well. Lara began
to wonder if all the crazy events of the past year had
just been a bad dream. It was such a relief not to have
to think about atomic bombs and bad guys traveling
through time.

Where did the Bench Guy go anyway? Well, she was
not going to worry about it. Isn't that what the expression "let sleeping dogs lie" implied? She would bide her
time, and thinking about that only made her chuckle.

She missed her dear friend Sujita though. She still
had her faith, it was as strong as ever, but she missed
hopping around the galaxy and seeing impromptu per-
formances by her Lord, Jesus Christ. It would be nice
to see all those mystical travelers again. She laughed just

thinking about Jesus's stand-up routine on Aravia's planet. And what about that audience music? What a show! The doorbell rang; it nearly made her heart jump a beat, she was that engrossed in her nostalgia.

"Hold on," she said to the person on the other side of the door. "Just a minute." Lara had to get some better clothes on. Her house was warm, but once she opened the door, she was going to feel a blast of cold air. Brr. January in the Midwest is no joke.

It was the weekend. Hubby and the boys had gone on an excursion to the dinosaur museum. Lara was just hanging with her dog, reading a good book. The dog did not lift her head at the doorbell. She was as peaceful as ever. That is strange, thought Lara. What the heck? Is the dog sick?

She opened the door, and to her surprise she saw her dear friend Sujita. And the front yard had disappeared. In its place Lara saw a vast garden, more like an arboretum. It was not cold, but pleasantly warm.

"Would you take a stroll with me?" Sujita said. Lara smiled with delight at the word *stroll*.

"You bet I would! Can I bring the dog?" This was so exciting.

"Absolutely, yes. And you may not realize it, but both you and the dog have been here before," Sujita said, as if this encounter were the most natural thing in the world.

"Oh, really? Where is here?" Lara was curious.

"Heaven." Lara's jaw dropped.

She looked back at her dog, and as she did so, Lara noticed that her clothes had changed. She was wearing a beautiful summer dress and sandals to match. She felt so stylish. What a welcome break from the bleak January day she had expected.

"Come," Lara commanded her dog, but the dog needed no command, she was already at the heel. "This *is* heaven," she chuckled. Her dog was not always that obedient; it was a welcome change.

Lara and Sujita walked for a while, neither of them speaking for some time. In this place it seemed wrong somehow to speak out loud about anything. It was that calm here.

Sujita broke the silence. "This is the last time you will see me. I had to say goodbye."

Lara was confused. If this was heaven, then wouldn't she see Sujita at the end of her life? And was Sujita dead? Lara said as much with her facial expression, if not with words.

"No, I have not died. At least not like you mean." Sujita read Lara's mind, just like always.

"Then what?" Lara queried.

"I think it is what you have learned about saints. I am not saying that I am a saint. It is just that my body will not be found on the earth. I have simply returned to my rightful home, intact, just as I am," Sujita was speaking, earnestly trying to help Lara understand.

"Oh, I see," Lara said. But she did not fully understand. If Sujita was like a saint, then she had to be in heaven, didn't she? "Oh, do you mean that even heaven is not heavenly enough for you? You are that good? Are you joining with Father God?" Lara said all this clumsily. She knew that she was missing the mark somehow, but it was the best that she could do.

Sujita was laughing. "Lara, you are amazing. Even when you do not know something for sure, your guess is close to the truth of the matter."

They were both laughing now. Lara could see that her friend was happy. If losing her identity was what Sujita wanted, then who was Lara to stand in her way? Sujita just wanted to join with God. It was that simple.

"I'll miss you, Sujita. More than you will ever know." Sujita laughed at that.

"I hardly think that I will not know how you are feeling." She kept laughing.

Lara laughed with her, once again. "I guess we will be the closest of friends then." It was beginning to dawn on Lara, the enormity of what Sujita was planning. When Lara prayed to God, Sujita would be there, listening. It was like a prayer group at church, only this team effort was on a scale hardly to be imagined.

They stood there, looking at one another. Once they said goodbye, they would never be able to stand next to each other again. It was a loss, and it was hard to see the gain of it.

"It's time," Sujita said.

"No, no, please. Just two more minutes." But Lara knew it was time, whatever that meant. She had to let go. She never felt more alone. She had just found this fellow mystic traveler, and now she was supposed to let her go.

Lara found herself crying the most heartfelt of tears. She had never known a goodbye that was more bittersweet. How many times had she wished she could hug God, almost join him? But she had always imagined that she would continue to be who she was. Yet her friend did not have that kind of limiting imagination; she was willing to lose herself completely in order to gain everything.

Would this spiritual learning curve never cease? Lara would have gladly lived an entire lifetime and not known this kind of pain. Yet the pain she felt. Growing was painful, yet she found herself constantly doing it. Was she a glutton for punishment? But she had to focus on the here and now. Even here in heaven, she had to discipline her heart, mind, and soul. It was time.

"Lara, I love you and I will always love you." Even Sujita was crying now. Maybe it took saying goodbye to realize the enormity of her loss too. She knew what she was gaining, but now she was experiencing firsthand the loss.

"And what about the time-travel mystery? Is it still on? Or has that ended too?" Lara wondered.

"Your world has not changed, Lara. Which is why you still have to stay on the job." As she said this, she began to disappear. And Lara knew that this was it. This was the final goodbye.

"Please tell Father and Mother God that I love them and I will do my best. I promise." And just as Lara was saying that, she saw something spectacular. A blinding white light engulfed Sujita, and somehow it got a bit brighter. And then Lara heard Father/Mother/Sujita's reply.

"Peace be with you and your family, Lara. Always." And the light was gone.

CHAPTER TWENTY-EIGHT

ANNIHILATION

Lara found herself lying down on her couch with her warm, furry dog curled up alongside her tummy. She cuddled deep into her dog's fur, she and the dog moaning with contentment after their heavenly experience together. She was crying sweet tears, remembering her friend Sujita. Never in her life had she thought it possible to unite with God so completely as Sujita had. It was shocking to realize that she may have the option to let go of her identity. She always pictured living out eternity as herself.

This new option, that of complete surrender, even to the point of annihilation, opened up a gush of gratitude on Lara's part. Her identity was a gift from God, and he was willing to let her be herself for all eternity. He would not end Lara's life; he was willing to let her exist for always.

Lara could let go of everything on this earth, but the thought of letting go of her eternal life in heaven made her feel uncomfortable. And that feeling made her even more empathetic to people here on earth. Because for some people, the thought of letting go of their *earthly* life made *them* feel uncomfortable. She could well understand their reluctance to develop their faith now! They wanted to stay where they were at and not grow. They wanted to avoid that kind of pain, and who could blame them?!

Lara wanted to punch God in the nose sometimes. He was making her grow in all sorts of ways, once again. And it was painful, to say the least. But she was the wiser for it. She needed to grow and learn in order to do her mystic traveler job well. He was pruning Lara so that she would become stronger and healthier.

She needed to learn this lesson. That everyone had to walk their own spiritual path, and that they were allotted whatever amount of time they needed in order to fulfill their destiny. Within reason, of course. And therein lies the crux of the matter, time. It was all about time, and she knew that time was always running out.

The phone rang. Lara did not want to answer it; she just wanted to lie on the couch and take a nap and stop maturing. But duty calls, literally.

"Hello?" she answered.

"The set is all ready, Lara." It was the agent. His voice was smooth as velvet, but did she detect a crack in it?

"Okay. Great. Do you need me for anything?" He went on explaining details and arrangements. She was to fly out on spring break. That way she could oversee the tone and content more fully.

When she hung up, she sighed. She was apprehensive about this California trip. Who and what would be waiting for her there was worrying Lara. The agent could not be trusted. And Lara wondered about the NRA staffers whom she had overheard talking about the conspiracy. She felt exposed somehow.

The agent had sounded a tad bit anxious on the phone. Were things going wrong on his end? Did they blame her? She would soon find out.

She prayed.

"We're home," she heard her husband say as he and the children walked in the back door. They were so excited about the dinosaur museum and the new exhibit there. Lara was glad to hear the details. This was her life, and she was going to enjoy it. It was a gift, for sure!

As the twins were playing with their new toys from the gift shop, Adam took Lara aside. He was worried. "There was a mass shooting nearby. Are you okay?"

"Yes, I wasn't aware of any trouble." She was surprised to hear about such violence so close to home.

"Crime, nationwide, has skyrocketed. Do you think there is some connection between the crime rate and the time-travel mystery?" Lara's eyes opened wide.

"Maybe that is the nudge. Maybe somehow the guns hold the key. Could they be giving people a subliminal message?" He shrugged. But Lara was forming an idea so ghastly that she knew it was probably true.

"I don't see how," he answered.

But Lara knew something that her husband did not know. She had mentioned a couple of times in the past that she could hear animals and plants talk. Like telepathy, she could hear them speak to her in her mind. But she had never talked much about it because it was something that even her family found hard to believe.

But what she never told her husband was that she had an inkling that she could hear inanimate objects speak as well. She found this hard to process, so she had just decided to ignore this ability. It was one thing to be clairaudient with life forms, but really, inanimate objects? She had to draw the line somewhere, for her own sanity.

"We need a babysitter," she said with resolve.

"Why?" But Adam knew that look. Whatever was going on, it was going to be done in a hurry. And somehow he knew that it was his fault because he had mentioned the mass shooting.

CHAPTER TWENTY-NINE

LORD OF THE TIME TRAVELERS

Lara called her dependable nanny service. "Can you get me a babysitter in the next thirty to sixty minutes or so?" She was holding her breath. Would there be a babysitter available at such short notice?

If only she could get her hands on the weapon used in that mass shooting. Or even just get close enough to listen to the rifle. She dare not say her plan out loud, even to her husband. It sounded too dangerous and out there to be coming from a sane person. And she knew she was sane. She waited.

"Yes, it just so happens that I have a college student available. She is eager to get jobs. I will call her and get back to you ASAP." Lara was so grateful that she could have cried. If she was finally onto the nudge aspect of the mystery, then she was that much closer to solving this crime before it hurt more people.

Adam had a contact in the local police department. They met him at the crime scene. Somehow he had managed to get Adam and Lara up to the crime scene tape. Lara kept her gaze down and tried not to speak to anybody. She let Adam make small talk with his friend, a retired military veteran.

"Adam, it's been a long time. So funny that you reach out to me now, under these circumstances. But I guess I could use a little support right now. These mass shootings are beginning to wear me down. I feel like I am back at the war zone." His name was Fred. Lara could tell he was worn down, confiding his vulnerability to his long-lost friend.

Lara thought of the police officers who took their lives after the January 6 insurrection. Knowing everything she knew, she was rightfully worried about these police officers' mental health. Something more needed to be done to help police officers nationwide. They were hit from all angles. Most of them were trying to do a good job, yet conforming to the somewhat racist system, but trying nevertheless to break the mold. It was an uphill battle, and they were literally fighting for their lives.

Lara spotted a black-colored weapon. Not knowing anything much about weapons, at least not as much as Adam, she was only able to say, "Is that the rifle that was used?"

Fred was surprised that Lara showed an interest in the scene. He had thought Adam had brought his wife along reluctantly. Maybe she was active military too. He did not know. Maybe his wife had an interest in law enforcement.

"Yes, yes, it is. As you may know, this type of weapon obliterates its victims. It blows them into pieces. It's a messy, gruesome scene," he said somewhat matter-of-factly.

Lara knew only too well the end result of using such a weapon. She had been on the receiving end, mostly during her medical training, of many a gunshot victim. The lucky ones who survived needed extensive surgery to repair the gaping wounds. Sometimes the law enforcement officers responding to the scene were woefully outgunned, and they risked their own lives when trying to save these victims.

Practiced at quieting her mind, letting calm seep into her body and soul, Lara began to listen. This was Adam's cue to distract his police officer friend. He made chitchat and began to show photos from his smartphone of their children and their antics.

A peaceful scene unfolded before Lara's eyes. She was back on Aravia's planet. The purple colors and the beach once again enveloped her with their strange beauty. She looked around for Aravia but saw no one. Soon she began to hear a lovely melody.

"Laaaarrrraaa, Laaaaaarrraaa." The song went on and on, building upon itself. And then she saw him, the singer. He was a handsome figure, half-dressed, showing an almost bare chest. And he was Indian, Lara was sure of it. Could Sujita be around too? But she knew better than to wish for that.

The stranger stopped singing and looked at Lara, not speaking or gesturing but standing there like a god. Patiently waiting for Lara to reply to his greeting song.

Finally Lara realized she must speak. It was quiet, so peaceful, almost like that heavenly experience she had had with Sujita, but she must find the courage to speak.

"Lord?" She did not know him really, but clearly, he was on the side of goodness and he carried himself with authority.

"You speak truth. I am Narada. The one who has been sending you back in time." Lara was stunned. She realized in a flash that the divine was much more complicated than she had previously thought. It was hard enough to have faith and develop a relationship with her Lord and Savior, Jesus Christ. But now she was to accept other Lords of goodness, Indian gods at that. She bowed, but he gestured for her to stop.

"Lord? What is it? Why are we here together? Is this next step a difficult one? I was trying to hear an inanimate object. I guess what I was thinking was far fetched." Lara was unsure what this all meant. She was overwhelmed.

"We have the gift of traveling through time and to other realms and worlds. I brought you hear to lessen the impact of what you will hear. You must be brave, Lara. Seeing is believing." And he was gone.

Lara sat on the sand, listening to the waves lap gently against the shore. She focused on that sound until she was in a deeper trance than she had ever experienced before. The sound deepened, and it became prolonged. It lost its distinction as a wave. Soon the only sound she could perceive was a deep hum. She listened even closer to this hum. She began to slow her thoughts and mind to match the cadence of this sound.

It was deep and slow. So slow that she realized that it was possible that what she was hearing was a word. A word spoken so slowly that it almost became a hum. Finally, after listening to this deep hum for a rather long time, she had an inkling as to what the word might be.

"Kill." It was barely a word; it was more like a deep chant, and the word seemed to never end. Kkkkkkkkiiiiiiiiillllllllllll. On and on it went.

Although Lara was sitting on the sand, and she knew that she was sitting on the beach, she began to feel as though she were in other places. Her empathy deepened and she saw scene after scene of mass shootings. Explosions of fire bombarded her eyes. The smell of burned flesh scorched her nostrils. The loud bang of gunfire was unmistakable.

Lara saw children screaming for their lives. She heard mothers crying and wailing. She saw countless funerals and men, mostly young men, behind bars. She saw police cars giving chase. The sound of their sirens becoming her heartbeat. Her chest was heaving with panic and anguish.

"Lara, Lara." It was her husband. He was shaking her. Fred and Adam were looking at Lara as though she were a ghost. And no wonder. Her skin had turned to an ashen color. Beads of sweat were running down her forehead and stinging her eyes. She needed medical help and fast.

CHAPTER THIRTY

BROKEN HEART SYNDROME AND HOLLYWOOD

Lara woke up groggy. Through bright hospital lights she saw her worried husband, asleep in the chair beside her bed. How long had she been unconscious? What had happened?

She remembered Aravia's planet, that was a nice memory. And she had met the divine lord in charge of managing all her time-travel excursions, or at least most of them. She knew for sure that she had initiated that visit to her husband in Europe.

"My love, how are you?" Adam was waking up too.

"I feel fine. When can I go home?" He was laughing. Just like Lara to speak plainly and with an action on her mind.

"You *are* fine." He laughed.

Chuckling, Lara said, "Why am I here though?"

"Believe it or not, you had broken heart syndrome. They call it takotsubo cardiomyopathy." Lara was astonished. Never in her life did she think that she would have any sort of heart condition.

"When you came out of your trance, you began to complain of chest pain. And I could see your breathing was not right. They said that broken heart syndrome is more common in females and people over the age of fifty. You have both risk factors. Also during the pandemic, you got depression. They say that that puts you at higher risk too." Lara understood what her husband was saying; he wanted her to slow down and not risk a recurrence of this condition.

"Did I get any complications from it or am I okay now?" She knew it was possible to completely recover from this. And she sure did not plan to empathize with countless mass shooting victims, all at the same time, again. She shuddered to remove the thoughts; she did not want to strain her heart again.

"No. Your heart cath was completely normal. There were no blood clots. Your blood pressure is so low that they do not even recommend putting you on a medicine to reduce strain on your heart. You're going to have to just avoid stress." He practically ordered Lara to take it easy.

"Great. Then let's pray." She held her husband's hand; she knew that only God could help her avoid this type of heart strain again. He had better listen to their prayers. This time it was Lara giving the command.

Adam and Lara sat in silence, each thinking their own profound thoughts. Lara had explained everything that she had heard and seen to Adam. Sitting in the hospital room with her husband, she felt completely safe and taken care of. She knew that her kids were happy and safe too. She sighed deeply.

"How in the world did aliens figure out how to make metal *talk*?" As Adam spoke, he realized that his question answered itself. "Ah. Out-of-this-world technology."

"Exactly," Lara said.

"Looks like the bad guys concentrated on promoting hell in that laboratory of theirs, not heaven. Chaos and destruction on earth foot the bill more than peace." Lara agreed with her husband's assessment.

"Yep. The military-industrial complex benefits from war, not peace. American weapons are sold to many different countries throughout the entire world. Unfortunately, America is spreading death, not democracy." Adam, too, agreed.

"Do you think that the NRA is in cahoots with the military-industrial complex?" Adam was putting it all together.

"Guns and white supremacy have long been intertwined. And the military has its fair share of white supremacists, trained to kill no less. And the illegal militias, those people are prime targets for radicalization. They must respond well to subliminal messages that already match their inclination for violence and domination."

Lara really wanted to go back to Virginia. If only she could get into that laboratory. But the California trip was looming near. For some reason, though, she knew that California held important clues to this time-travel mystery.

"Oh my gosh." Adam was startled, and for a moment he thought Lara was in trouble medically again.

"Do you think that Hollywood is in on it too?" Even as Lara said it, she knew that she was probably right. It all fit together now. The agent. The far right. The military.

"Well, we had better find out, hadn't we? But first, you lie back and rest. Doctor's orders." He smiled his most charming smile. He knew that Lara would do as she was told if he poured it on, and it worked. She sighed deeply and laid her head down and fell into a peaceful sleep.

CHAPTER THIRTY-ONE

BLEEDING KANSAS

It's California or bust. Spring break had arrived, and the entire family was on board to head out to the golden state. The twins had Disneyland and fishing on the Pacific Ocean in mind. Adam was thinking about protecting his family; he was hoping for the best but fearing the worst. Lara was thinking about her book being made into a Netflix series; she was hoping the adaptation was true to the gestalt of her first fruits as an author.

The Southern California weather was balmy and comfortable, a welcome change from the harsh winds of Kansas. But Los Angeles was so crowded. Lara did not relish staying in cities; it was nice to visit them, but not some place she would like to call home. She liked big, open country and an unobstructed view of the starry night sky. But she could see that Los Angeles had a lot to offer despite its obvious drawbacks.

There was so much history here. Los Angeles had a significant amount of seventeenth-century Spanish Colonial architecture. That amazed Lara. The weight of history, and the greed that came along with it, was palpable here.

Kansas, on the other hand, did not have that much recorded history. Basically Kansas history started in the mid-nineteenth century. Native Americans had occupied the entire state of Kansas prior to the white man's arrival, of course, but there was not much documentation or recorded history to speak of regarding that earlier occupation of the land.

There were a few exceptions. There was a bit of a ruin in Kansas from an early Spanish explorer. Lara loved visiting the Coronado Heights Castle in Saline County, Kansas. Funny to use the word *height* in any description of Kansas! In reality, it is a small hill, about three hundred feet high, surrounded by vast grassland prairie. The Spanish explorer's name was Francisco Vázquez de Coronado (c. 1510–1554). He was a governor of the province New Spain (Mexico). He led a major Spanish expedition up Mexico's western coast and into the region that is now the southwestern United States in 1540. He was looking for gold, but he decided to stop his expedition in Kansas. If only he had not given up and kept heading toward California and Alaska. How would that have changed history? Lara wondered.

The castle overlooks the Smoky Hill River, and it gives a view of 230 million years of geological history.

The ancient saltwater sea that used to cover the area left a mixture of marine, fresh water, and subtropical fossil material. But, in modern times, the surrounding countryside is covered with grasses and nearby wildflowers. The area immediate to the hill has a few different species of trees. Maybe that is why the Spanish conquistador thought it ideal for a settlement.

Unlike California, where the weight of history pressed on Lara's mind, in Kansas, when Lara had first arrived some years ago now, her psychic impression had been that of death. The bison (commonly called buffalo) were killed in the millions over a very short period of time in the nineteenth century. They were not killed for any good purpose really. The white man wanted to get rid of the buffalo so that the Native Americans had no sustenance. And it had the added benefit of clearing the land for their cattle.

Then of course, as all schoolchildren learn when studying history in school, Kansas got its name as "Bleeding Kansas" because leading up to the Civil War, there had been such bloody battles between the settlers who were against slavery and the white settlers who were for slavery that some say that the Civil War really started in Kansas.

This got Lara thinking about Kansas today. It was necessary to go back to the Civil War to find a period of time that the United States of America was as politically divided as they are today. Kansas had just recently been the first state to push back against the United

States Supreme Court *Dobbs* decision of June 24, 2022. It was August 2, 2022, when Kansas voters decided to say no to an amendment to the state constitution that would make it more difficult to choose an abortion and access reproductive health care.

Was Kansas, once again, the harbinger of war to come? Was another civil war on the horizon? No one could argue that Kansas was a liberal-leaning state, but Kansas certainly had a knack for choosing the right side of history when push came to shove.

Lara wondered, is that why God had chosen her for this time-travel mystery? Because she was a Kansan? Was Kansas supposed to point the way, was it destined to play a pivotal role in preventing another Civil War? Lara sure hoped so.

Lara recollected her impression when she had first met the professor. She had thought she was not too far from home during that time-travel journey to the 1950s airport. Los Alamos, New Mexico, is not far from the Wichita, Kansas, area, where Lara now lived. Nowadays, it would take only ten hours to drive to Los Alamos, where the professor had developed the world's first atomic bomb. But Professor Oppenheimer could have easily flown a plane to an airport in Kansas. It is highly possible that he had come to Wichita's airport directly from Los Alamos.

Lara knew that the McConnell Air Force Base, where her husband was stationed, was built in 1951. And she had thought that her time-travel excursion to meet the professor was during the 1950s. But she also knew that the area where the air force base is located was used as an airfield for a few decades before 1951.

That got her thinking about Fort Riley. It was an army base in Kansas that had its origin as far back as 1853. Could this time-travel mystery be related to events on *that* base?

But she had no time to ponder this idea any further. "Look at that!" her husband said as the Pacific Ocean came into view. She and her family were in their rideshare, headed toward the hotel. The sights and sounds were too interesting to allow any further contemplation on Lara's part. It was time to focus on this new region of the country, the glitzy state of California, where hopeful actors go to make it big.

CHAPTER THIRTY-TWO

A CLOSE RESEMBLANCE

"My warm-weather wardrobe is sorely lacking. Can I go shopping while you guys go to Disneyland? I can meet you there later. There are shops outside the theme park gates, but those may be expensive. I can check out the local strip mall first; I like Dress for Less and Marshalls. Lots of dresses there." And Lara was thinking of shoes too. But she did not want to overwhelm her husband and talk about that. He was loath to do any shopping himself.

"Just come quickly, I will miss you lots," Adam said truly enough.

"Great. Anything you and the boys need while I am out?" Unlike Adam, Lara enjoyed shopping. Carrying the packages was her only worry.

"Nope." Adam kissed his enthusiastic wife goodbye, and she was out the door to catch a rideshare.

The independence of going out alone was welcome to Lara. One day, soon enough, the kids would be grown and gone, but for now she had very little alone time. She sighed deeply. Soon her rideshare dropped her at the strip mall. She immersed herself in checking out racks and racks of dresses. Being an easy size six, and a bit taller than most women, Lara always found it rather easy to find clothes that fit. She learned long ago that she must discipline herself and not buy everything that she liked. Over the course of many years, she managed to keep her closet a bit on the sparse side. She dared not accumulate too many clothes. But even a smaller wardrobe needs refreshing every now and then.

She was looking intently at a few choice dresses in her favorite color, blue. Next to Lara on the right was a middle-aged Indian woman. She was shorter than Lara and had a bit of a waist, but there was something glowing about her.

"Excuse me, I do not mean to be rude, but you look so much like an old friend of mine. She was so beautiful." Lara was thinking of Sujita. Having connected with Sujita so deeply, Lara had learned that Sujita was from a different time than her own. And Lara knew that Sujita had been a medical student.

The woman turned to face Lara. Lara was stunned to see her face in its entirety. She could have been Sujita's twin or very closely related anyway.

"How did you know your friend?" It was nice of the lady to make conversation with Lara. She could have moved on, but she lingered to chat.

"She and I met for the first time in a very large classroom. Actually, it was more like a show than a lecture," Lara chuckled. The Indian woman could see that Lara had many happy memories with her dear friend.

"What was her name?" The lady continued the conversation.

"Sujita." The lady turned pale; she was that struck at hearing the name.

"Oh my. Are you all right?" Lara was practically carrying the woman to a nearby seat. "Is there anything you need, maybe some water?"

"Yes, let me rest just a moment. I have not heard that name in ever so long." Lara now realized that she was the cause for this kind lady's near collapse. She wanted to make it right, but she had no idea what to do other than to stay by this lady's side.

After a few minutes of silence, Lara could see that this lady's normal color had returned. The woman took a few sips of water from her water bottle. She smiled once again.

"I am sorry. I was not expecting *that* name." She shook her head sadly. "I had thought I would never hear that name again."

"Oh, I see. Did you know a Sujita as well?" Lara still had no idea of what was to come, she was that preoccupied by this lady's possible medical condition.

"Why yes, Sujita was my sister." Oh. Lara now realized the truth. Sujita had had a sister! No wonder the resemblance was that strong!

"May I ask what your name is? My name is Lara." This time Lara extended her hand out to give a proper introduction. Both ladies were now past their initial shock.

"So nice to meet you, Lara. My name is Sujata." They both smiled at that. Some parents liked to have fun with kids' names. It must have been a bit confusing growing up; maybe they had nicknames to help avoid chaos in the house.

Lara liked talking with Sujata; they became fast friends. They both realized they were famished and decided to eat at the Thai restaurant located in the same strip mall. When Lara had texted Adam, he knew that this was no coincidence, meeting Sujita's sister. He agreed to watch the boys as long as she needed to be away. Plus, he let Lara know that Disneyland was fantastic, and he was enjoying himself immensely.

Lara and Sujata were laughing and chitchatting as if they had known each other for many years. They began to learn about one another. It turns out that Sujata had never married. Like her sister, Sujita, she had also gone to medical school. Once she was done with her studies, she and her parents had immigrated to the United States. They all lived together in a nice condominium not far from the strip mall. She was a practicing gynecologist and her parents had just recently retired.

"So, how did you know your Sujita?" She still did not know the truth.

"Well, as I said, we met in a large classroom. But I did spend time visiting her in her hometown. It was called Pune." Lara had to think a moment to let the name of the town come to her mind. It was a practiced deep knowing.

"Oh," was all that Sujata could say.

"Is that where you are from?" Lara knew that she had to help her new friend. Sujata was obviously not a mystic traveler like her sister had been. If Lara told Sujata everything, it would be a tremendous shock. She knew that she had better keep it light, let the conversation flow naturally over time (Lara knew it was all about timing).

"Yes, do you think your friend and my sister were one and the same person? Did you study in India with my sister?" It was an incredible coincidence; Sujata was so far from home, she never thought that she would meet someone who knew her sister.

"My friend left this earth as a young woman. It was my honor to know her as long as I did. She had a spiritual gift; she was very devout." Sujata was nodding her head vigorously.

"Sujita had so much to offer the world. It was a shame her life was taken so young." Sujata was silent for a moment, no doubt deep in thought. She hung her head and said, with barely a whisper, "My brother

Pavan was convicted of her murder. He went to prison for what he had done."

"Oh no. I am so sorry that happened to your family." Lara now realized that this conversation was taking a terrible turn. It was bad enough to lose her friend the way she had, but Sujita's poor sister had no idea about the good thing that had happened to Sujita. She mistakenly thought that her sister's life was taken by an evil act, and by her very own flesh and blood! Lara knew that at the very least, she had to set the record straight for Sujata. This was no easy task. So much to unravel here.

Sujata was shedding tears of regret. She explained how her brother Pavan had gotten in with the wrong crowd. He had had a gambling addiction and he was also a heavy drinker. He had brought so much dishonor to the family. And then when Sujita had disappeared, witnesses at the medical campus had said that Pavan's friend Kunal had been seen manhandling her.

"They never did find Kunal, but the authorities put two and two together. Pavan was sentenced to prison for life. He was spared the death penalty only because they never found Sujita's body. They knew it was all circumstantial, but it had to be him." Lara had immediate compassion for Pavan. In a way, Sujita's disappearance was probably partly his fault. But she also knew that Sujita was not murdered.

"Where is your brother now? Were you able to visit him in prison?" Not knowing why, Lara felt sure that

Pavan knew the Bench Guy. And Lara was pretty sure that the Bench Guy's name was Kunal.

"Somehow he got out of prison early. I think on good behavior, although that is hard to believe. He also came to the United States. But I am not sure how that was possible since he was a convicted felon. He became a citizen and joined the United States military. He is currently stationed in Kansas."

Lara's jaw dropped. Impossible, she thought. But deep down, she knew that her new friend was telling the truth.

CHAPTER THIRTY-THREE

FINDING A NUGGET

When Lara finally met up with her family at Disneyland, she was somewhat distracted.

"What is it?" her husband asked.

"You won't believe it; you just won't believe it," she said, trying to take it all in herself.

Adam knew that there was no point talking about it now, and from Lara's expression, it was clear that the news could wait. In fact, it probably should wait. All he could do was lead the family in fun for the rest of the evening. There were fireworks later on, and he sure needed to see those. Maybe mind-blowing news would sink in better if he did.

Lara and Adam were turning in. It had been a long day. The hotel room was quiet and peaceful; although the suite was not quite cleaned up from the tornado of fun that they had had throughout the day, it was at least manageable. Lara liked to clean and straighten up.

She was good at it. But she knew that talking with her husband and getting a good night's rest were more important right now.

After Lara explained everything, he lay there in silence, dumbstruck. "So all roads lead to Kansas."

"Damn, even when things don't look good, you still make me laugh." Lara never swore, so Adam knew she was letting off steam. But in a way that could help her cope, with humor.

The Rome analogy did not bode well with Lara. Didn't their civilization end up collapsing? More and more Lara was thinking about powerful forces, powers that be that wanted chaos and destruction. She knew that the United States was bitterly divided. Divisions that had been stoked by Trump and his white nationalist and Christian nationalist allies.

White men in rural areas were the demographic most likely to own a gun. It seemed that many of those people had been negatively influenced by the ugly subliminal message that the guns contained. And it was not just gun owners in the United States. Looks like the weapons, any weapons, made by the conspirators within the military-industrial complex, had the capacity to nudge people into killing.

Kill. It was a powerful command. Succinct and to the point. Temptingly simple. In a complicated world, one that is difficult to navigate with its fast pace and conflicting tensions, it certainly would be a relief to have something straightforward to explain it all. Or at least, to take an action that was straightforward anyway. Evidently some people believe that killing other people would solve their problems.

"But what does India have to do with all of this?" Adam was thinking it all through. "And how could the Bench Guy be Indian? He seemed like he was of European descent. But I guess that is pretty stupid of me to even articulate, since in reality, he was an alien."

"Yep, I guess if he can change into a white guy, then he can change into an Indian guy just as easily. And there is another thing I was thinking. When I go back in time, sometimes I get the feeling that people around me see me as someone else. Like I do not look like myself. Maybe when the Bench Guy, or should I say Kunal, travels through time and space, he will always look like the part he is playing."

She put this idea on a mental list to ask the Lord Narada about. Now that she knew who was managing the time-travel excursions, at least *her* time-travel excursions, she realized that she could get a lot of her questions answered. Finally.

"Not to use too many famous quotes here, but do you think the force runs strong in Sujita's family? Maybe that is the Indian connection? You had to know Sujita so that you could also know Pavan? And I guess also Sujata?" Adam was trying to piece it all together. It made sense. But then Lara wondered what else Pavan and Kunal had been up to in India.

It could not be just a circumstantial murder case that had sent Pavan to prison. There had to be more. And Lara was determined to figure it all out. But first things first, she was set to meet the agent tomorrow. Why and how was Hollywood involved in this potentially worldwide conspiracy? That was Lara's next clue, and she was not going to leave California without finding that most important nugget of information!

"Well, I guess it's fitting that we are in California," Adam said with a smile. "Because you're my pot of gold somewhere over the rainbow."

"It's 'at the end of the rainbow' and no more Kansas jokes!" she begged.

"I'll stop, if you start." She immediately reached for his scrotum and pulled hard.

"I'm taking hold of your golden nuggets, lover, and I ain't never letting go!"

Adam was thanking God almighty for sending his wife on this dangerous mission. The more dangerous it got, the more he got. He fully supported all of his wife's endeavors as a mystic traveler.

CHAPTER THIRTY-FOUR

THE FOX'S LAIR

It was decided that Adam would take the twins on a fishing trip while Lara went to Hollywood. Lara would miss having that fishing adventure. She loved the open seas and hanging out in nature. But she also knew that this was a working vacation. Not only was she focused on solving the time-travel mystery, but she really wanted her book made into a successful Netflix series too. She had to put in some time on the set.

They were all about to head out of the door when Lara's phone rang.

"Lara, I think that you told me you were going to Hollywood today? Today is my day off. I have to bring my father to the doctor in the afternoon, but I have time to hang out with you until then. Is it possible for me to accompany you?" Lara was surprised to get a call from Sujata. It had not occurred to Lara to invite a friend to the set.

"Sure, I guess that would be all right. But may I ask why you are interested? Wouldn't it be a bit boring for you?" Lara was genuinely curious.

"Well, you see, my father is a big Bollywood fan. He has never toured Hollywood, and he was wondering if he might accompany us?" Now Lara was beginning to understand. For her, this was work. But for others, it was a chance to immerse themselves in the glamour of the movies.

"Ah. I see. That makes perfect sense. Let me check with the agent to make sure bringing guests is okay and whether or not they can accommodate a group. I will get right back to you." Lara was not at all experienced with the correct etiquette of movie production. She did know that Bollywood was a big deal for a lot of people, and that Bombay (now Mumbai) was the Indian equivalent of our Hollywood. When she called the agent, he was not at all surprised at the question; his answer was immediate.

"Of course. How many will be in your party?" Lara was relieved that this change in plans was so easy to do. The agent assured her that the guests would not interfere with their work; he had people in place to keep them busy. She expressed appropriate gratitude and assured him that she would be arriving early.

They arrived in separate vehicles since Sujata was leaving early to bring her father to the doctor. Lara was grateful for the companionship. She realized that it was a bit nerve racking embarking on this new venture into filmmaking. She was confident in her style and vision, but it was nice to bounce things off a friend, even a new friend like Sujata. And Sujata's father, an enthusiastic and impartial observer, would also be a welcome support on her first day at work in Hollywood.

All smiles, the three of them finished going through the security screening process. Their hostess led them through well-appointed corridors and glamorous-looking conference rooms until they were finally brought to a comfortable lounge. There was no one else in the large space; it had all the amenities that Sujata and her father would need. The hostess started detailing the tour that she had planned for Lara's companions. Sujata's father was open eyed and eager.

The door opened and in walked the agent. Lara recognized him immediately, and she also knew one of his assistants. It was the assassin lady. Lara recoiled inwardly, but she kept a neutral countenance. She did not know the agent's second assistant. He was a middle-aged Indian man, but he was fit and handsome. Lara could not take her eyes off of him, he was that alluring.

Next to Lara, Sujata seemed alarmed. Between her and the male assistant, Lara was not sure where to hold her attention. Lara was vaguely aware of Sujata's father. He was busy looking at the TV screens, so he did not take notice of the newcomers as Sujata had.

The entire group of people fell silent. The tension was palpable. The agent was genuinely shocked to see Sujata. It was he that broke the silence first.

"Lara, you never cease to surprise me. This is an unexpected turn of events." Unlike Lara, the agent knew that Pavan's family lived in the area. But he had never dreamed that the family would be reunited on his movie set.

"I see that some introductions are not necessary," Lara said with a smile. She was quick to recover from her shock at meeting Pavan. He was the agent's second companion, and an unexpected one, to say the least.

"It is my pleasure to meet you for the first time, Pavan, even if you certainly do know my friends here." Lara held out her hand.

Pavan was a man of the world, certainly shrewd and mature. But did Lara detect a flicker of hope in his eyes? Sujita was his best friend as a boy. Maybe some of that childhood innocence remained inside of him somewhere, buried deep.

Clearly he decided to play along. "Lara, it is a pleasure. And I owe you a debt of gratitude for gathering this group together today. How can I ever repay you?" Lara could not tell what Pavan meant. His words were kind enough, but they almost sounded like a threat.

She knew that she could not wait for the next shoe to drop. She had to take action. Sujata and her father had to know that danger was near. Just knowing Pavan's past was sufficient to perceive that much. But Lara knew more then they that the agent, the assassin lady, and Pavan were all on the bad guy team. And unfortunately, Lara and her new friends were trapped in their lair.

CHAPTER THIRTY-FIVE

SOMEWHERE IN BETWEEN

"Hold my hand," Lara commanded. Sujata reached for Lara's right hand; at the same time, she grabbed her dad's left arm.

Lara had only initiated time travel once on her own. She hoped and prayed she could do it under pressure. With practiced ease, she entered a meditative state. She was determined to get the hell out of there. Sujata had no idea what was going on, but she was on Lara's side for sure.

It took a moment, but Pavan recognized what Lara was trying to do. It was a remote memory, but he recalled that Sujita had taught him a bit about her time-travel skills. Just as Lara was about to disappear, he reached for her left hand. The agent and the assassin lady followed suit; they grabbed onto Pavan.

"No!" Lara yelled. She yanked hard at her left hand, but Pavan held it firmly.

It was too late. The entire group of six was disappearing into thin air. In an instant, the lounge was empty.

Lara found the journey through time difficult; she was being pulled and pushed, all at the same time. No one dared let go of their grasp on the other; the heaviness and drag seemed to be carried mostly by Lara. But she did not let go of her focus. As difficult as it was for her, at least in comparison to her previous journeys, she could sense that the others were having it even worse. Even in that moment, her ability to empathize with others was still strong. She recalled that it takes a while to get used to time travel. Probably the others were nauseous and weakened from the dragging sensation.

The peaceful in-between place came into view. It was just as Lara had remembered it, only more beautiful. As the others were getting their bearings, Lara was bracing to meet the devil. But she looked around and saw no one else. Relieved, she made sure to start separating herself from Pavan and leading Sujata and her dad away from the bad guys. She had no plan, but she knew that she needed to distance herself from them.

It was the agent who recovered first. "So Kunal was right. Time travel really is possible." He was well pleased. He knew about the doors, and he knew about the access he might have to other times and places.

Unlike Sujita, Lara was more of a fighter. She may not have had the same level of faith as Sujita, but she had grit. She pulled a small knife out of her ankle holster.

"Don't come near us! I know how to use this thing." She could see that Pavan was bracing for a fight. The assassin lady, too, was recovering from her nausea. Just as Lara was wondering how in the world she could fight them both off, she heard a heavenly voice. They all heard it.

"That door. India." Was Lara imagining it, or did that voice sound an awful lot like Sujita's? It was almost like the time that she heard the word *Virginia*. But it wasn't Sujita's voice; it was something more.

Lara did not need another moment to obey the godly command. She pulled Sujata toward herself and said, "I know this is hard to believe, but you have got to go back home."

"What?! Why? Where?" Poor Sujata, thought Lara.

"No time to explain. Sujita will show you the way. It is time to have faith, Sujata. You must be brave." And as Lara said that, she pushed Sujata and her father through the nearby door.

But as she did so, the assassin lady grabbed onto her. As they were fighting, the agent guffawed.

"I know what we shall do, Lara. Let's fix this situation before it even has a chance to start." And as Lara pushed off the assassin lady, he dragged her away from Lara and pushed her in front of another door.

"What are you doing? Are you mad?" And Lara knew that the assassin lady was right. The agent really was mad; he was out of his mind with a lust for ultimate power.

"Kill Lara. You will find her on the beach. It is all her fault that Kunal is gone. She must pay!" And as he said that, he sent the assassin lady through another door.

Somehow Lara knew that the assassin lady was sent back to that same beach in the Caribbean where they had first met. And she could see now why the assassin lady was so angry. She blamed Lara for everything that was going badly for her and the bad guy team. The assassin lady had no choice but to obey this new devil-in-charge.

As the agent was gloating, and clearly reveling in his newfound role of taking charge of time, Lara was left to battle Pavan.

"Don't do this, Pavan. You're better than this," Lara said, but at the same time, she was bracing for a fight.

"Don't do what? You don't know me." He was circling Lara. He realized that she was more powerful than expected. He was not sure how to get out of here, but he knew that Lara, and maybe the agent, did know a way. He was hedging his bets.

"I know that you got in with the wrong crowd. You made mistakes. But it wasn't your fault that Sujita left." Pavan was surprised. He put it all together, and in a flash, he realized that Lara was speaking the truth. She was a mystic traveler. He knew that now. And he also knew that Lara and his sister must have been friends.

Lara could see that Pavan was thinking. She knew it was now or never. When she looked around, she could see that one door seemed brighter than the others. She knew that was her ticket. She ran at top speed for the door.

If the agent had been paying attention to her, then all would have been lost. But for some reason, the agent was enthralled by the white, heavenly in-between place. Lara had no idea how the agent could gain so much power, so quickly. But she could not worry about that now. And anyway, it was to her advantage that she only had to contend with Pavan.

Pavan seemed to make up his mind. He chose to follow Lara. Like Lara, he began to run at top speed. He wasn't sure that he could go through a door on his own. And anyway, he wasn't sure how to choose the correct door in the first place.

Lara could see that Pavan was at her heels. It was unclear what his intentions were, but she couldn't take any chances. She ran to save her life. Just as she pushed to fall through the door, Pavan lunged and managed to catch Lara by the ankle. She kicked and resisted but it was futile. They both fell back into the same lounge that they had left only minutes before.

"Get off me," Lara yelled. They fought each other, not knowing why and to what end. The agent was gone. The assassin lady would be defeated back in time. Pavan's sister and father were safe.

They both separated from each other, taking a gasp of air.

"I'll never follow you," Pavan said, but Lara knew that he had done just that. He was conflicted. But she couldn't convince him of anything in the heat of the moment. She had to get back to her family. She had to leave him behind.

"I don't know what you are going to do, Pavan. But I'm leaving." And Lara walked out of the lounge, leaving him behind.

CHAPTER THIRTY-SIX

SUDDEN GOOD FORTUNE

Lara was hurrying to her car in the studio parking lot when she heard Candy. "Dr. Tigler, please don't go."

Surprised, Lara turned around. "Candy?"

"I am so sorry the agent and his staff left precipitously. Very unexpected. But his assistant assures me that the show must and can go on," she said with a smile as she was closing the distance between them. She, too, seemed out of breath. Clearly, Pavan had the presence of mind to recover quickly from their time-travel experience; he was a man of decision after all. And Lara was pretty sure he hadn't made a sudden leap to join the good side of the force.

"Well, the agent..."

"I know. He should be here. But all the necessary documents are in hand. There really is nothing stopping you from enjoying the fruits of your labor." Lara thought about it a moment; clearly Pavan had made provisions for her. It did not give Lara a warm-and-fuzzy feeling to know that Pavan was that intricately involved in the time-travel mystery and her book-made-TV-series production. Somehow Lara knew she was being manipulated. She had no doubt in her mind that Pavan was returning to Kansas, and he was preparing for their next meeting. Shivers ran down Lara's spine.

"Of course. I was just going to take a moment to contact my family. Give me ten minutes, and I will rejoin you in the studio." Candy acquiesced and returned to the building.

Please pick up, please pick up, Lara was thinking as she dialed her husband's phone, safe and sound in her air-conditioned car. She could hear the phone ringing on his end. Not much time had passed since she had left the hotel. Maybe she could still catch them.

"Hello." Lara was never gladder to hear Adam's voice.

"My love, do you have a moment?" She could hear the twins giggling and playing in the background. It sounded like they were outside.

"Yes, definitely. We are at the dock and the guide has toys and games to occupy the boys. This is going to be great." Lara smiled. How she wished she could be as carefree as the twins.

Lara filled her husband in. He was greatly surprised, not so much that Pavan was a bad guy and stayed a bad guy, but that the agent turned into some sort of devil.

And Sujita helped his wife from heaven, or wherever she lived now. His faith was strong, but he was the first to admit that the divine seemed kind of complicated and mysterious.

"I guess the best thing to do is to go back inside. I have a job to do here. But I am itching to get back to Kansas." She did not know what exactly was waiting for her back home. But she had a feeling it was something big.

"Let's take one day at a time. Just remember to pray, Lara. That is the main thing." They gave each other the usual goodbyes. Each knowing how precious their love was and what a gift it was to enjoy this life!

As they hung up, Lara obeyed her husband's wise words immediately. She prayed and prayed, until finally she felt centered once again. She was ready to go back inside the studio.

Her phone rang. "Lara?" It was Sujata of all people.

"Sujata! How glad I am to hear your voice. Are you and your father all right?" Sujata proceeded to fill Lara in. This time it was Lara who was amazed. God, or really Lara, had sent them back to their country of origin. But it was the present day. Sujata and her dad had been there a week already. They had a house and a car and even servants.

"Yes, more than all right. The community here seems to accept us, and it is as if we have always been here. The servants seem to think that we go back and forth to North America. I talked with my mother by phone. I convinced her to come back to India. She was shocked that dad and I were here, of course. But all I could do was tell her the truth. Sujita had a hand in it. And it is a good thing she did. Because Mom's brother is very sick; she needs to come visit him." It was a lot to take in, but Lara was so happy for Sujata.

"Would you check on my mother before you go home? I can send you the information." It was an easy matter to answer in the affirmative.

"Of course, Sujata. It would be my pleasure." They promised to keep in touch. Well, thought Lara, that conversation certainly brightened my spirits. Leave it to God to answer a prayer!

CHAPTER THIRTY-SEVEN

A TIMELY DEPARTURE

Lara enjoyed filmmaking immensely. It was a privilege and a pleasure to be so intimately involved with the creative process. She found the entire Netflix team to be professional and devoted. Also, they fed her well, which was much appreciated.

At lunchtime, much of the crew had wanted to return to the same lounge where she had met the agent and his assistants. She had agreed, but reluctantly.

When she was in the lounge, she replayed the morning's confrontation in her mind. She was glad for Sujita's family. Lara had wanted to make it right for them; they had lost so much in the past. But God had made the crooked places straight in his own way. He had provided, and it was good!

Pavan seemed a lost cause though, and that was sad. But the thing she worried about the most was the agent. He seemed to lose his mind almost instantly upon arriving at the in-between place. And when was she going to see the assassin lady again?

"Hey Doc, we've gotten a lot done today. The rest of today's work is procedural kind of stuff. If you want, you can head out and do some touristy things?" Lara was only too happy to call it a day. Yes, she could think of a lot of things to occupy her time in sun-filled Southern California. She expressed her gratitude and promised to be back first thing in the morning.

As Lara was getting into her car, she thought of Sujata's mother. She would drive straight there and check on her. Maybe she could help her pack.

Lara walked into the condominium's lobby. She was happy to see that security had a strong presence there. She started making chitchat with the receptionist.

"Yes, I see that you are on the visitor log, Dr. Tigler, yes. I will have a security officer escort you to the elevator. How are you related to Dr. Patel? You are listed as a family friend. You must be a very close friend. They rarely have visitors." Lara lingered. She understood that Sujata and her parents had been careful through the years, not trusting many people.

"You are almost in time to see Dr. Patel's brother. He is expected shortly." Lara thanked her lucky stars that she was not one to procrastinate. Thank God she had come right away. Now if only she could get Mrs. Patel to agree to leave immediately and without her son, Pavan.

"How nice," Lara said. But inwardly, she was anxious not to see him. She must act quickly.

When Lara met Mrs. Patel, she knew instantly that all would be well. Mrs. Patel seemed eager to leave.

"Lara, so nice to meet you. I had thought I might see my son; it has been so long. But I fear that it would be unwise. Perhaps we should go." Lara could not agree more. She was all for family reunions, but this hardly seemed like a good time.

They closed up the condominium and Mrs. Patel was safely seated in Lara's vehicle. It was a relief to drive away.

"We have hired a professional house sitter. I will miss my friends, but I have to admit I am excited to go back home." She was beaming from ear to ear.

"You will be back, Mrs. Patel. But apparently, the gods have plans for you and your family in India." Mrs. Patel smiled at Lara. She heard the word "gods" and knew that it could not be easy for Lara to come to terms with Indian mythology. It was so nice to sit next to Lara, knowing that she had an intimate connection to her long-lost daughter.

"Is Sujita happy?" Lara could see that Mrs. Patel was putting a brave face on everything, but she wanted to know that her daughter was all right, even with the Creator!

This time it was Lara that laughed. How the tide had turned. Sujita had laughed when Lara showed concern about surrendering so completely to God. Now it was Lara's turn to see the bright side.

"She is with the Creator, Mrs. Patel." Lara said it in such a way as to make it obvious to this worried mother that all was well.

"Of course. And that was her choice. I respect that. But I miss my little girl!" They both laughed at that. Knowing that it was true, and it would always be true. There was a special place in heaven for mothers, everybody knew that.

CHAPTER THIRTY-EIGHT

THE WORLD'S MOST BEAUTIFUL AIRPORT

Mrs. Patel's plane flew off into the sunset. She was taking the route over the Pacific Ocean toward India. It would be a long journey, but she was ready for it. She had her United States passport as well as her Indian documentation. Her family would be there to pick her up once she reached her final destination. She welcomed the chance to be alone and think about her entire family and her faith.

Never had the gods been more real to her than they were right now. She beamed with pride thinking about her faithful daughter, Sujita. She had never felt very close to Brahma, the Creator. Now she wondered if that was a mistake. Now, more than ever, she was eager to know the Creator. After all, she needed to check up on her daughter.

She was almost laughing out loud now.

That made her think of Lara. What a delightful woman. Lara seemed exceptionally faithful. She knew that Lara was a Christian. Did that mean that Christianity was also a true religion? Was Jesus Christ the Lord and Savior of the entire world? Just as she had heard?

In the past, she had thought that the Christian religion was so much nonsense. It seemed violent and useless to her. Now she was not so sure.

It was time to get off the plane; she was in Singapore for a stopover. She was eager to stretch her legs and see this world-renowned airport. She was heading for the forestlike gardens and the waterfall. The lights on the ceilings looked magnificent in and of themselves.

The overhead speaker said, "You have arrived in the Changi Airport..."

As far as Mrs. Patel was concerned, she had arrived in paradise. It was beautiful. She wanted to splurge and visit an "outdoor" café. The food was delicious. Did she still have time to catch her plane? She thought so. She wanted to check out the hedge mazes and maybe even the animal-shaped topiary garden.

She was walking through mist, a cloudlike effect that made her feel so relaxed. Children were playing on a nearby oversize sculpture. Their laughter made her think of her children while their family was still together, all those years ago now. She was becoming more comfortable with Sujita's destiny, but when thinking of Pavan, she began to frown.

Surely he could be saved. She prayed as she hurried toward the hedge maze, breathing in the fresh and misty air.

She went deep into the maze. She had always been good about directions; it was her gift. She was not afraid to be alone or that she might get lost.

"She is getting close. I'm worried." It was a deep voice, a voice Mrs. Patel had never heard before. She held perfectly still.

"This is almost over. So what if she gets in the lab? We'll be ready." She heard footsteps and the men seemed to have left the area.

But Mrs. Patel did not move a muscle. In front of her stood her beautiful daughter, Sujita. But she was like a vision. She was not human really.

"Oh." She was struck with wonder.

"Tell Lara what you know. All is well." She winked.

"Can Pavan be saved?" Why her mind shifted to her son all of a sudden, she did not know. Her daughter was not quite her daughter any longer, but her heart was swelling with joy at having seen her at last.

"Of course. Anyone can, except those who have chosen otherwise. Some souls will never turn." She spoke so beautifully. Mrs. Patel wished she would come back, but she knew that would never happen.

"You make it sound so simple. Life is difficult." Mrs. Patel spoke with almost a bitterness, a bitterness that she knew Sujita would never have.

The figure shifted into a more human-shaped form. It was a man that she did not recognize. His eyes had compassion and love in them. He seemed to understand her regret and pain. His handsome face turned to sadness, and she saw a tear drop from his eye. The tear turned into a puddle, and the puddle turned into a pond, and the pond turned into a lake, and finally, the tear had become a vast ocean of pain. Mrs. Patel looked down into that ocean and she saw the earth. It was covered in pain and sorrow. He reached his hand into the ocean and lifted the earth out of the depths. It dripped, but it seemed to dry quickly in the light of his face.

He was beaming with happiness. He looked at her and came forward. "Courage, dear one. All will be well." The vision disappeared and she was alone in the hedges once again.

CHAPTER THIRTY-NINE

THE HOLLYWOOD CONNECTION

"**I** insist that you slow down." It was Adam. A lot had happened in California.

"You need to pace yourself. Remember what happened at the crime scene?" He was right. As anxious as Lara was to return to Kansas, she also had to be in the moment. She had to take care of the task(s) at hand. And right now, she was wrapping up her work on the movie set. With the agent gone, it was actually fun. His presence was always a creepy reminder of ugliness and corruption. It was nice to be able to throw herself into some creative work for a change and not have to think of anything else.

Medicine was an art, but it was not meant to bring out someone's creative side. Day by day it was arduous and high pressure; the stakes were high in the medical world. Why not enjoy and watch her literary work undergo the process of coming to life on people's screens?

Also, she had to admit she was not regretting that the assassin lady had been sent back in time on a fool's errand. The past would be keeping her busy for a moment. It was nice that both she and the agent would temporarily be off their game. They may have had a good working relationship, who knows, but certainly it would take some time for them to come to terms with their newfound access and dominion.

Of course she knew time was a bit on the tricky side, but even space and time had a cadence. Pavan, too, had to be adjusting to the recent change in his circumstances. She had no doubt that the bad guys would regroup, but for now she felt a pause was warranted.

"You are right, love. You're right. Let's enjoy that date tonight." They had arranged a babysitting service to watch the children in the hotel room. The boys were looking forward to popcorn and a movie.

"Are you going on a date, Mommy?" Isaiah was always so supportive of his parents spending time with one another.

"Which dress are you going to wear? The purple one?" And Jacob was always complimenting Mommy when she wore pretty dresses.

"I love you two so much!" Lara gushed as she bent down to hug and kiss them. Of course that made them recoil and run away.

"Mom!" they both said in unison. Lara knew that they didn't want a kiss; they were too busy gathering their toys so that they could show them to the new babysitter.

"Yes, the purple one." Lara went to change and do her makeup. She heard the knock on the hotel room door.

A kindly middle-aged woman was at the door. Adam and the twins were introducing themselves. Lara stepped out and Adam swooned.

"I only have eyes for you." He practically sang those words. And it was true. He was ready to leave. It was left to Lara to update the babysitter on what the twins may or may not need for the evening. But Lara was practiced at communicating with the nanny back home, it was like second nature.

"Have fun. And please feel free to call me as often as you need to. I will send you photos and updates." It was good of the babysitter to reassure them. They closed the hotel room door behind them and both took a deep breath.

"Where to?" Lara always loved it when Adam took charge of the dates. He was especially good at choosing comedy shows.

"Ballroom dancing," he said. Lara was surprised but pleased. She was glad that she was wearing her comfortable heels.

"I know I told you not to think about the mystery, but I found an event that is something like a far-right fundraiser. Being from Kansas, I thought that perhaps we might fit right in." They both laughed. They were devout Christians, and they were a military family, but fitting in might not be so easy in some cases.

"Perfect. Let's dance the night away and hear what our fellow Americans are plotting." Laughing, they were on their way.

As they were driving, Adam explained that dinner and dancing would be at the fundraiser, and then he had booked some tickets at a comedy show. He knew that she would appreciate the chance to dance.

"So what is the fundraiser for anyway?" He explained that his military friend's wife had some tickets to an Academy of Motion Picture Arts and Sciences membership meeting. This particular banquet was just for the executive branch of the academy.

"I guess her father is an executive in the industry." Lara was thrilled. She could have hugged her husband right then. She was curious if she would find a clue at this special dinner event. Every clue and insight were helpful in flushing out the purpose and ultimate aim of the human-alien conspiracy.

The hotel was fancy. They were ushered into the banquet hall, and immediately exquisite chandeliers caught their attention. The centerpieces on the tables were elaborate. It was simply gorgeous.

The food was divine. To their surprise, no one questioned them about their lack of high-level involvement in the industry. When making small talk with their tablemates, if anything, the others at the table seemed well pleased that there were fresh faces in the mix.

"Shall we dance?" said her romantic husband.

"Yes, we shall," Lara said just as formally. And they joined fingertips and stepped onto the dance floor as though they were performers at a ballroom dance competition on PBS. What a night.

Adam was turning Lara, and she was responding to his direction nicely, when they both had the sensation that they had stepped back in time. Lara came around to face her husband and she could tell that the banquet hall had changed.

"Lord Narada is at it again," she said. But they did not miss a beat. They took the time to look around and saw that the faces were changed. They were nearly all white. The style of dress seemed most consistent with the 1940s.

"I remember that Professor Oppenheimer studied at Berkeley in California. No, I'm sorry, he taught physics at UC Berkeley from 1929 to 1943. Do you think it is possible that he might be here?" Professor Oppenheimer was the only connection to California during the 1940s that she knew of, but he lived and worked in Northern California. It was doubtful that he would have an opportunity to come down to Southern California. Lara did not remember reading that Oppenheimer had any important visits to Los Angeles.

"Oh my gosh. I don't believe it." Lara wondered what Adam could have meant. But it was obvious that he wanted her to follow his gaze.

"Kunal? Here?" She was stunned. He really got around.

"Just act natural. He saw my face and he did not bat an eye. It is possible that Lord Narada wants us to learn something about Kunal and his plans. You said that when you first met him, he had thought that you were a mystic traveler. Do you think that it was fate to meet him here? Now?" Lara was truly clueless about Lord Narada's exact intentions. But she looked at Adam, and he looked different. She was sure that she looked different as well. She did not see why Kunal had to know who she really was.

"I never got the idea that Narada worked in that way. It always seems more like he wants me to eavesdrop or engage with others to learn certain important facts about the time-travel mystery. He seems to have more straightforward intentions." Adam nodded. He was thinking it was nice to be in disguise for a change.

When they got back to their table, they were not surprised to see Kunal and a companion sitting there. They smiled as a greeting. That was all they could do to recognize their tablemates. Another speech was beginning.

The man at the podium was distinguished and clearly a well-respected leader. The banquet hall fell silent, anticipating his every word.

"We know our audience, don't we?" he was saying. Everybody was chuckling, if not outright laughing. Lara and Adam were not in on the joke.

"So in order to reach our ultimate goal, we need to keep to the same pattern. We want to increase gun sales and build confidence," he went on, speaking about details specific to the movie industry. He was recounting tried-and-true strategies to keep movies pumping out the same successful plan of action.

He had only mentioned the word "gun" once, but it was enough to startle Lara and Adam. They did not dare speak with one another. They could not afford to tip their hand. Clearly, participants in this meeting were all of the same mind.

When the speech was done and people were returning to the dance floor, Adam again asked Lara to dance. Only this time he seemed almost desperate to get out of his seat. Lara was feeling sick to her stomach.

"Yes, let's," she answered with as much enthusiasm as she could muster.

They barely moved, but they swayed a bit, trying to keep to the rhythm. Thankfully Lord Narada had mercy. He brought them back to the present time.

"It's time to laugh, Lara." She could not have agreed more. It was time to head for that comedy show.

CHAPTER FORTY

MAUNDY THURSDAY

As the family was boarding the plane to return to Kansas, they could see the news on the TV console in the waiting area for their gate.

"Mommy, what's happening?" said Isaiah.

"I don't know, honey." But Lara did know. At least she thought she knew. It felt like the heat was on, maybe literally. The weapons had been made with the kill command for so long now, for decades, that the subliminal message contained within them had finally culminated in a mass action of violence. Even the news anchor reporting the violent events around the country, the world, seemed puzzled. What the heck was happening? Civilization was getting more advanced and sophisticated. Love seemed ever more embraced and accepted. It just didn't make sense that there should be this much backlash.

Lara and Adam looked at one another. Although they had known that this trip to California was much needed on many levels, they were both eager to get back home. They should make it home in time. But for what? It seemed like the country was heating up inside a pressure cooker, and it was about to blow.

The plane ride was uneventful. The kids handled it well, as always, being seasoned travelers due to frequent military moves and visiting family around the country. Nevertheless, it was with relief that they stepped into the Wichita airport. Being a relatively small airport, it was easy to navigate. It was always clean and the people were nice. But not today.

The various workers in the airport seemed tense. While the family was waiting for their luggage, Adam checked his news feed on his smartphone. His frown deepened.

"What?" Lara was afraid to ask.

"The main highway headed home is closed. There was a multicar police chase and it ended badly."

Lara put on a fresh smile for the children. "Hey guys, let's take the surface streets home."

The boys cheered. Whenever she brought them to Exploration Place, their favorite children's museum, she tried to drop off the dog at the doggie day care for playtime. When she and the boys would pick her up, Lara would always ask them which way home they preferred. And almost always, they liked the surface streets. Granted, it was a bit odd to ask the boys this question leaving from the airport. But they took it as their same old game.

Lara was relieved.

The sunshine and prairie grass swaying in the breeze was welcome to their scorched eyes. Southern California was gorgeous, almost fake looking, but there was something authentically beautiful about the grasslands of the prairie. It was easy on the eyes, no need to strain through smog and high-rise buildings to see the land. Already perfect, there was no need to landscape an artificial ambience.

The mood lifted in the truck. Lara checked her weather app. "Oh no, big storm on the way." They all knew what that meant. Turn on the weather radio and listen for the tornado siren warning. Why did tornadoes always seem to occur at night? But it was a necessary precaution. They knew what to do.

"Let's have some hot chocolate when we get home," Adam said helpfully. They all smiled.

They fell back into their routine. The storm was strong, but no siren blared. Maybe their sleep could have been more restful, but they were ready for the new day.

Lara received a text from her husband the next day; she took a moment to step away from her desk at work. He had off Good Friday. They could all go to the Fort Riley army base that weekend. And his dad would be joining the family, just like he did every Easter holiday. From January to May, Lara's mother-in-law was not available, as she was a CPA working eighteen-hour days. Lara enjoyed spoiling her father-in-law. She would feed him an Easter dinner to remember, and he got to play the Easter bunny for the boys. Only this time, they would all be staying in a Holiday Inn near the army base. With a pool of course.

They would take the same highway that they usually took to get to Kansas City, only at El Dorado, they would veer left onto Highway 77 and go straight north to the army base. It was a shame not to visit Lindsborg, but they could visit Florence and Junction City on the way to the army base. Lara loved checking out new municipalities. Although her favorite small town in Kansas had to be Lindsborg. Unfortunately, they would not be going that far west. Only 3,700 or so people lived in Lindsborg, but the town had really catered to tourists with a charming main street that featured uniquely decorated Dala horses. And they held a Svensk Hyllningsfest biennially. The large Swedish population gave the town a European flavor, a nice connection to the old world.

Later, when Lara told the boys about their weekend excursion, they had many questions. "Will we see the castle ruins?"

Lara laughed. "No, we're not going to the town with that special playground." They were disappointed. They associated the El Coronado ruins with the very large neighborhood playground just off the main street in Lindsborg.

"But we are sure to find more playgrounds along our route. And Daddy booked a hotel with a pool." She smiled and tucked them into bed that night. Let them dream about adventures, Lara thought. The cosmos was full of special places like the beach and playground on Aravia's planet. But good old planet earth was full of special places as well.

Grandpa Tigler arrived safely on Thursday. The family had one night to pack and get ready for their excursion. Holy Week was always a special time for the family. And of all their relatives, Papa was the most devout and enthusiastic about attending the nightly services. Of course he had arrived early in the day so that the family could attend the evening service together.

The twins thought it funny that the priest washed their feet. Holy Thursday is commemorated annually on the Thursday before Easter. Called Maundy Thursday, it was a special and unique service where the priest humbled himself in front of the entire congregation and washed everyone's feet. It was fun to see everybody's socks. Some of the ladies wore special socks just to get a smile from their friends. But it was a reverent event, mimicking the time when Jesus washed his disciples' feet to make sure they knew that he was there to serve, not to be adored per se.

Spiritually satiated, the family went to bed that night hoping for a great weekend. Lara and Adam were just hoping for a safe and uneventful weekend. But somehow they knew that their hopes would be dashed.

CHAPTER FORTY-ONE

JUMP IN

Isaiah and Jacob were used to Mommy and Daddy preparing for the worst. They were a little surprised that their parents were packing both cars, though, and with so much stuff they would probably never use.

"Mommy, are we going to eat all these meals?" It was Isaiah. Her little soldier. The family had fun eating the meals-ready-to-eat (MREs) while camping. Of course they would catch their own fish and eat food they had brought along, but it was good practice to get the kids used to MREs.

"Are we going to use all these weapons, Mommy?" Part of Isaiah was excited and part of him was worried.

"Think of this trip as a practice run," she said with a wink.

"It's good to do a dry run, even if we don't use this stuff. But I do want you to be ready, baby. You need to fill your backpack with important tools." Isaiah understood. Some of their camping trips were in remote areas of national parks. It was important to be able to survive if lost. Also, if needed, it was important to be able to defend oneself.

"Okay, Mommy. I'll be ready for the bad guys." Yes, Lara thought, let's be ready.

It was a pleasure to see Papa again. He was entertaining the kids, but he could not help but notice that Lara and Adam were making, what seemed to him, quite unnecessary preparations for a weekend trip. And on Easter weekend at that.

"Am I missing something?" If you only knew, thought Lara. In the very back of her mind, Lara wondered if he did know. Something, anyway.

"We thought we would take two vehicles. In case we want to do separate excursions and for convenience." He nodded. But he let Adam run his own family. He just wanted to be the grandpa.

Adam was gathering the group together, including Mitzie, the dog. "Okay everybody. We're not going to stop at Andover or El Dorado. We're headed straight for Junction City. It's only a few miles away from the army base."

"Is there a pool?" Obviously, that was the most important question of the day, at least in Jacob's mind.

"You bet. And we're hoping to do some hiking on the Flint Hills Nature Trail. There is a rock that is three thousand feet tall; it is called Castle Rock." The twins were amazed. That seemed awfully tall to them. Their eyes were used to the vast flatlands of the prairie, so any hill or mountain was a welcome change.

In the past, Lara used to do some rock climbing. In answer to her husband's gaze, she nodded ever so gently. Yes, she had brought her rock climbing gear. He nodded back approvingly.

It was a fun caravan. The sun was shining, like it almost always was. The only thing that broke the rays of sunshine in Kansas were storms. And it was a clear day.

In a couple of hours, they checked into their hotel. Naturally, swimming was top priority upon arrival. Lara knew that she needed to swim. She had to loosen her core and rid herself of some built-up tension. She had to be ready for whatever came her way. It was a gift that Papa was there. She was able to focus on laps and getting a workout of sorts while Grandpa played with the children.

And the Jacuzzi was welcome to her back muscles. She prayed and meditated. She breathed. Adam could see that his wife was preparing mentally. He, too, was inwardly doing a mental checklist. Did he prepare his family adequately? Would they be able to defend themselves if a civil war broke out? He had a few nature books. He knew that Lara was a good forager. She would be able to survive on the various plants. And Mitzie was his reliable hunting dog. But the weather app showed a storm brewing in the west. It was headed for Kansas. Storms could be deadly. They had to remain vigilant.

Lara and Adam had a few moments to themselves in the Jacuzzi. "Did you bring the weather radios?" Lara asked, picturing herself cranking and cranking to charge the device. If cell phone coverage became unreliable for some reason, then those weather radios could save their lives.

"Yes. And I got you the updated fob for my truck. Just in case, for some reason, you need it." Lara smiled. He was always making sure that she had what she needed. She kissed him.

"I'm hoping that they don't do a 100 percent ID check at the gate." Adam knew what she was thinking.

"We all have the same last name. We have to accept that they know you are coming," Adam said wisely.

"Nevertheless, I will be a passenger. Let's just hope that they don't check the cargo area of the truck," she chuckled.

"I know. That would not be good." Adam resigned himself. It was what it was. They had to take the chance and bring weapons on base. Never did he think that he would enter any military base with the intent to fight off his own comrades. It was criminal.

"Let's go," Lara said with conviction. "Let's do this."

Lara and Adam took the double meaning. They jumped back into the pool, and it was frigid.

CHAPTER FORTY-TWO

BETRAYAL

Entering the army base was without incident. All of their miliary IDs were scanned and accepted. They did check Lara's ID, but it did not seem to make a difference one way or the other. Of course, appearances can be deceiving.

Papa had some contacts on the base. He wanted to meet them at the bar in the community center. But he had some time to kill beforehand. Lara and Papa were always keen on exercising together. Unlike Adam, who hated exercise, they seemed to revel in it. Adam exercised more than they did, but he preferred to run and lift weights in the early mornings before work. Well, that was fine. He could bring the boys to one of the many playgrounds on the base while Lara and Papa did their thing.

They drove off in different directions. Lara had her truck. Her favorite vehicle was an F-150, and Jeep was a close second. The truck had four-wheel drive and could handle almost any kind of weather. Plus it was comfortable and spacious, which suited a large man like Papa.

"What a beautiful day." She would take in the sunshine, never knowing how long it would last. She thought she saw a storm brewing in the west.

"So, what do you think? Elliptical?" Of course they would start with the elliptical machine. They would not have it any other way.

"Let's go for it," Lara said with unabashed enthusiasm. She was ready to hit the gym hard. After the elliptical machine, they would do weights. Papa would be cheering her on and she would be answering any medical questions that he may have.

It was Good Friday. They had called ahead, and the gym had limited hours. But they had made it in time. To their surprise though, the gym was nearly empty.

"Wow, that's strange," said Papa.

"Why? Do you think it should be busier?" He nodded in the affirmative.

"Well, let's count our lucky stars that we have this opportunity." As soon as he said that, dozens of well-armed men came charging into the gym.

Lara and Papa reacted swiftly. They hopped off their machines and made a dash around some of the equipment. They made their way to the free weights. Papa gave Lara a signal to pick up some weights to use as leverage against the men.

"What's this about?" he said in his most commanding voice. Being retired military, he knew that this was not usual protocol and highly irregular. He sensed danger.

"Drop the weights," said a masked leader. In fact, all of the men were masked, which was odd.

"Leave my father-in-law out of this. It's me you want." Papa looked at Lara. What in the world could she mean?

"Too late, Mrs. T.," said one of the men.

"This is much bigger than any one man. No one will be spared," said the leader. And with that, Lara and Papa were led away. But first the men took the extra precaution to cover their heads with black hoods. Their hands were tied behind their backs.

Adam heard the signal on his walkie-talkie. He took it off his waist belt with dread. He had hoped that all of their many precautions would not be necessary. But as he looked at the walkie-talkie, he could not see any more lights or signal. No one was talking on the other end.

Oh my gosh, he thought. They have my wife. He seethed inside. But he did not show his anger.

"Come on, boys. We'll meet Mommy and Grandpa outside of the army base." He was met with questioning looks, but the twins knew that they had no other option than to obey their father's command. They were leaving.

Adam could not know where his wife was. But he knew that she had managed to give him the signal that something was wrong. She was not to push the button on the walkie-talkie unless something dreadful had occurred.

What had happened was that Lara had hidden the walkie-talkie in her workout towel. When the soldiers had come into the gym, she gave the signal. She left her walkie-talkie under the towel in the cupholder, hoping against hope that the soldiers would not check it. And they never did.

Lara and Papa were in a vehicle of some sort; it was a rough ride. Lara lost track of the turns. Directions were never her strong suit. All she could hope for was that Papa was faring better than she was. She had no way to know how he was doing. If they even tried to move an inch, the soldiers would beat them with some sort of a stick. She quickly learned to sit motionless. Or at least as motionless as one could sit while swerving in a fast-moving vehicle. She knew that she would have countless bruises in the next few days.

She had had a few X-rays done in the past few years. Sometimes she would get injured accidentally from her kids, sometimes she caused the injury by playing outdoor games that no middle-aged woman should be playing, but nevertheless, she knew from experience that her bones were strong. So far at least, no broken bones. Thank God for small favors, she thought.

And that made her think of praying. She willed herself into a peaceful state of mind. She prayed earnestly. All she could remember to say was the Lord's Prayer. But she thanked God that she had memorized it and chanted it over and over again all these years. Because that one prayer seemed to unlock some sort of key in her mind.

The swaying of the vehicle began to turn into the rhythm of the ocean waves. The bumps of the road turned into a breeze moving her hair, as if she was on a sailboat.

She opened her eyes and there was Jesus Christ, sitting in front of her. They were on a boat, sailing in the ocean. She thought of the boats that he had been on with his disciples thousands of years ago. She saw fishing nets lying on the floor of the boat. But it was his appearance that most struck Lara. He had no top on. His trunk was clearly visible, and he had multiple bruises all over his body. It looked like he had been beaten with a blunt object.

He was not smiling. He looked haggard but purposeful.

"This is what you have been training for, Lara. These men must be stopped. Love is on the move." And with that, she woke up into the present reality. She was once again in the military vehicle. She could feel a fresh hit from the baton that one of the men carried. She knew that she had not moved. It was obvious that the men were beginning to enjoy the opportunity to be cruel. She recalled seeing that the men had had plenty of guns and ammunition on them when they had stormed into the gym. No doubt the subliminal message of "kill" was resonating strongly with them.

She tried to silence her groans. Just as she was beginning to wonder how long the car ride was going to last, she felt the vehicle make an abrupt stop. She was unceremoniously pulled from the vehicle and pushed through some sort of elevator door. She sensed that her father-in-law was still with her. For that she was grateful. Now she wished she had clued him in on the danger. It wasn't fair that he didn't know what they were up against.

She felt a blow to her head, and she went unconscious. It was many hours later when she finally awoke. The black hood was still over her face and head. She was terribly thirsty. Her head ached badly. Her arms were stretched unnaturally backward. Her shoulders felt like they were ripping. She still had sensation in her fingertips, and she could swear that her fingers were touching her Papa's hand.

Groggily, and with a dry mouth, she managed to say something, "Papa. Papa?"

But there was no answer. She said his name a few more times. Still nothing. But then she realized that she could somehow manage to pinch his skin. Or at least she could try.

Her nails were not very long, but she tried her utmost to scratch her father-in-law. Scratch or pinch. Anything that might stimulate him.

"Ow." It was a soft grunt really. She tried again.

"Ow. You're hurting me." He had spoken louder. Good, it was working.

"Sorry, Papa. Sorry. It's me, Lara. We've been kidnapped." She could hear him trying to move. He was coming awake but much more slowly than Lara had. She hoped that he wasn't beaten too badly. She had better keep him talking.

At that moment the door swung open. Was it a heavy steel door? Lara wondered. A breeze flew into the room. It helped to freshen Lara's mind, and she hoped her father-in-law's mind too. She heard footsteps. They were heavy.

The door swung shut. Lara thought that several people must have entered the room. The air began to get stuffy again.

"Why are you here?" said a different voice, a softer tone. The soldiers were gone?

"Take this hood off and maybe I will tell you," Lara said brazenly.

Immediately she felt the hood being tugged off her head. The light was blinding. It took minutes to see clearly. She felt a glass being pushed to her lips. It was the best water that she had ever drunk in her entire life. She drank the entire glass of water.

When her vision returned to normal, she was stunned to see humans and aliens together in the room. The aliens were tall and pale. Their fingers were long, and their heads were very large in size. She wondered how Hollywood could have so accurately depicted their appearance all of these years. And then she realized that she already knew the answer to that question. Hollywood was in on it. They always were.

"How did you know I was the one?" Lara wanted to know. How had Kunal known that she was a mystic traveler?

"Haven't you guessed, Lara? Your father-in-law gave you away."

Lara could feel her insides squirming with nausea. She was that sick with a feeling of having been betrayed. She started dry heaving and then water and bile came out of her mouth.

Retching, she looked around, tugging on the bonds that connected her to Papa. She seemed to have no control over her own body; the reaction to the news was that visceral.

A man walked forward from the back of the room. Lara did not recognize him, but her father-in-law did.

"Parker," Papa said with resignation. He now knew that the alien had been right. He *had* betrayed Lara. He was looking straight at Parker.

"Well, I guess we won't be meeting later at that bar." The man shook his head.

Papa remembered many years ago that his son Adam had told him about Lara's time-travel experiences. It was only mentioned once and since Lara and Adam never mentioned it again, Papa had decided not to pursue the topic. But he also knew that Lara was saved.

A few years ago, when Parker had started befriending him, he had eventually told Parker about his daughter-in-law. His new friend had seemed curious about Christianity, like he was ready to convert. And Papa was always keen to convert others to Christianity. Lara's story of conversion as a young woman was compelling, and he thought that he would add in the mystical experiences to create drama. Now he wished that he was not so prone to embellishments and exaggeration.

In one devastating moment, he realized that his loose lips had brought them to this ruinous moment. He was crestfallen.

CHAPTER FORTY-THREE

SAINT PAUL'S ESCAPE

It was nice to be hood-free. But the air was stuffy. The lighting was low. The room was nearly empty and there were no windows. It didn't look good.

Lara was speechless. What could she say? Her father-in-law had played a role in the conspiracy. From the way that he had acted, she was fairly sure that his involvement was inadvertent. But it stung.

She was still tied to Papa, but she felt utterly alone. He would be thinking about the past and how he had gotten to this point. It would take him time to come to terms with what had happened. She wanted to admonish him for his foolishness in voting for a man like Trump. She wished that he had thought better of his misplaced loyalty to the right. He was blinded by the right and now he had ended up here, a victim of it. But she quickly let go of her bitter feelings as she realized that for all her comparative wisdom, she was sitting in the exact same room as her foolish father-in-law. She laughed out loud, realizing how ridiculous it always is to feel superior to someone else. It always comes to bite you in the end.

"Papa?" He stirred. It seemed like hours since the aliens had left them alone. They were getting weaker by the minute. No food. No water. They were lucky not to be sitting in their own waste.

"I thought you would never talk to me again," he said contritely. She winced. Hopefully he would never know her negative thoughts. It wasn't his fault. None of this was. It was no use playing the blame game. And wasn't that what the aliens were counting on anyway? They wanted humans to fight one another. They wanted humans to kill one another.

She now realized that the aliens' aim was probably much bigger than simply using earth's precious resources. What did that leader say? This was bigger than one man?

The aliens were planning to conquer the planet. That was their plan all along.

"Papa. Forget about it. Let's just concentrate on getting out of here." She could almost feel his relief. He was an amazingly strong man, slow to discernment, but once he knew the difference between right and wrong, he had no fear in fighting for the good guys. And Lara was clearly one of the good guys. His exceptional loyalty turned toward goodness; he was well on his way to becoming Jesus's disciple.

Lara had compassion for him. He had no idea, not yet, of how complicated the divine realm was and of what it meant to conquer evil. You got rid of one bad guy and a second later there was a new one to take his place. But thinking along those lines, Lara did not exactly have it right.

She did not know how much she had accomplished. Because of Lara, the bad guys were on the run, they were scattered, they were delayed. She had accomplished more during her time travels and forming the relationships that she had formed than she had realized.

But what she did understand is that she couldn't give up. And then she remembered Jesus's words. "Love is on the move."

"Papa. There is a way out of here. We've got to keep moving." He was aroused by her infectious enthusiasm.

"What are you thinking?" He sounded more like his old confident self. Good, Lara thought, they were going to have to use their wits and whatever amount of physical strength that they had left.

"This situation is impossible. I don't see a way out." He wasn't saying this statement to seem pessimistic. He was beginning to assess the situation and he was talking out loud in order to find a way. Lara and Papa were always a great team together. Now that he was all in, fighting the actual bad guys, Lara felt confident that they would get out of this situation alive.

"Matthew 19:26." This was it. This was the moment that all their years of being faithful were preparing them for. "With man this is impossible, but with God all things are possible." They knew this was it. Their faith would be tested in this moment. Lara and Papa had no way to escape, but with God's help, they would find a way.

"Remember Saint Paul's escape from prison? There was an earthquake and the doors of the prison fell away; they had prayed before that." Yes, Lara thought. And Saint Paul had converted one of the guards to Christianity. This was right up Papa's alley. She chuckled.

"Let's pray." And she and Papa began saying the Lord's Prayer. They took turns praying and talking to God. They couldn't tell you why, but they began to feel less thirsty, and they seemed stronger somehow, more like their old selves.

They heard the door begin to open. "Don't stop praying," said Papa. Okay, she thought.

They said the Lord's Prayer and pretty much ignored the guard. He was armed. Who knows what his plans were when he had entered the room, but he seemed genuinely surprised to see them in such great condition.

Lara felt compelled to tell the guard the truth. "The gun you're carrying has a poisonous message. It's controlling you. If you leave it outside the room, you'll think clearly."

Lara and Papa resumed praying. The guard lingered. He was confused, but he had time to think. The prayer that they were chanting was beginning to make sense to him. He remembered that years ago, he had known the difference between right and wrong. He knew that he was doing something wrong here, but it was hard to break away. He began to think about his childhood. His parents were loving, and the family gatherings were meaningful. He could see his mother's face in his mind; she was not happy with him for being here. She looked toward the door. The guard looked toward the door, half expecting to see his mother.

He left the room. Moments later he returned, and he was unarmed.

Lara and Papa kept praying. They conversed with one another and with God. They told each other godly stories. Soon the guard joined in. He was telling them about his family life and the church he sometimes attended as a youth.

The room seemed to fill with sunshine. The air was not as stuffy. There was a crack in the wall opposite the door. A ray of sunshine beamed into the room.

Not knowing why, the guard started talking about the building's layout. Lara found herself asking him about the whereabouts of the lab.

"Lab? I don't know what you mean." Lara was disappointed.

"Do the leaders go in a certain direction when they leave this building? Do they meet somewhere?" It was a long shot, but Lara was hoping against hope that she could find the lab. She felt certain that the source of the kill command was generated from within it.

"Oh, yes. They do head toward the HQ. Always. But me and my comrades, we never join them."

Lara's heart leaped for joy. "Help us find this HQ. Today you work for the Lord." The guard smiled. Without the gun, he was beginning to feel like his old self.

"I will. Thanks be to God." The guard looked at the wall. The gap of sunshine grew larger, and the three of them could see green bushes and a lawn spreading out before them. The zip ties on their wrists melted away. They stood up stiffly.

"No time like the present," Lara said, and as she said it, she led the men outside. They had to find firearms and she knew where to look.

CHAPTER FORTY-FOUR

OPPENHEIMER IN TIME

The three of them paused next to a large dumpster. "This is a blind spot. We should be okay for a moment," said the guard.

"I just need landmarks, then I can find the playground where Adam stashed the supplies." She was thinking of getting warm clothes. She was still wearing her scanty workout gear. She was looking forward to eating an MRE and freshening up, camping-style.

Papa's eyebrows went up in admiration. So Lara and Adam were preparing for this. Whatever this was. He knew Lara was not good with directions. It did not surprise him that Adam had schooled her on the map and had helped her by pointing out landmarks.

All this time, he had thought Lara was a "sheep." He had always felt like he was superior, he was the wolf. He was the free thinker. He knew what was best. The Left were a bunch of socialists, maybe even communists.

He never could figure Lara out. He had thought she was weak for supporting the lazy poor. She was misguided at best. But he knew that Lara never gave up; he could see that in her work ethic and how she was raising his grandchildren.

Up until now, her mysticism and faith were theoretical and almost fanciful. He could humor her. But now...

He winced. He was a fool; he could see that now. He almost laughed out loud realizing how very foolish he had been.

And now he could see plainly that Lara's faith was vastly greater than his. She was working for the Lord. She always was. And all this time, he had allowed himself to remain lost out of pride.

He shook it off. He was going to make up for lost time. He looked around. "I see the chapel. Did you and Adam orient yourselves with that landmark in mind?"

She saw it too. "Yes, if we are at the back door, looking right, about one block over there is the playground."

The guard spoke up. "We can't get to the church directly, but I know another way, one where we are unlikely to be seen."

They heard a thunderclap. The air was full of petrichor; they could almost smell the rain that was about to drench them. Lara shuddered. Spring in the Midwest was not exactly like a lamb. No matter what cliché you had heard.

"What day is it?" She mostly asked the guard since she and Papa were not likely to know for sure.

"Easter day." They all looked around their bleak surroundings. They were speechless. Not exactly how they had envisioned spending this day.

They set about following the guard. Papa watched him closely for signs of treachery. Lara watched the buildings closely, trying her best to follow the map in her head. She had to be sure for herself that they were on the right track.

Soon they came upon a playground. Lara could not see any signs of her family. She knew intellectually that they had been here two days prior, but she was hoping to see them. Even if it was just in a daydream.

She looked around, and she saw a marble on the ground. "This is Isaiah's, I just know it." She smiled. She was praying that her family was all right.

"It's going to be fine, Lara. Adam knows what he is doing." Lara so appreciated her Papa's optimism. That was just what she needed to hear.

"Over here," she called. She saw a bit of red color. Could it be the collapsible red wagon they had brought along?

They rushed behind some bushes; sure enough there were the supplies. And quite a lot of them.

"Wow," said the guard. Papa was not surprised. He had seen them preparing the vehicles for the trip and he had confidence in Adam. Things were packed nicely, just like Papa had taught his son.

"I see a fire. Over there. Someone is beckoning for us to come," the guard said earnestly. The rain began to fall. It fell in torrents. The wind kicked up. The clouds were almost black above them.

They looked around. All three of them saw troops closing in on them fast. On three sides, they were about to be surrounded. But behind them, there was a kind of woods. There was cover.

"The man near the fire is telling us to hurry," the guard spoke again.

Lara and Papa looked at each other. What to do? Could they trust the guard? Could this be a trap? They could not see the fire. Why would the guard be able to see it while they could not?

"What is your name, son?" Papa said in his most authoritative military tone.

"Raul." He said this as if nothing had changed. He did not seem to register their distrust and skepticism. He was without apparent guile.

Lara thought fast. "This is a test." She looked at Papa. He read her expression. He now understood the kind of almost daily pressure that Lara lived under being a mystic traveler. She was constantly being tested.

As if reading his mind, she said, "The Creator needs me to have faith. Faith is our primary means of communication. That is why he is constantly testing it."

Creator? Little did he know that Lara was changing her vernacular since meeting all her Hindu friends. By Creator did she mean God?

But he did not argue. Lara was speaking a little bit differently, but he knew that she must have meant

Father God. Of course he still did not know that the Father was one with the Mother. And he certainly did not know that a young Indian woman named Sujita was one with the Creator as well.

"Before we make a run for it, we must decide what to take. We need speed." Papa noticed that the troops were closing in.

"Firearms, ammunition, and communications should be our priority," said Raul. As he said that, he began to pick up what he could.

Lara simply grabbed the red wagon. It was full but she was used to pulling it when it had two large boys in it, so she did not mind the heavy weight. She began to run toward the trees.

Soon Papa and Raul passed her by. Raul was the fastest of the group. He hurried them along. "They are almost upon us. Just a few more steps to safety."

All three of them ran with all their might. The heavy rain pounded against their eyes. All Lara could do was pull and run. She gave it her all. It seemed the grassy field between the playground and the trees was the longest run she had ever made. But in reality, it was probably only a few hundred yards. Her chest began to hurt. Her breathing was heavy.

The darkness of the storm and the torrential rain gave them some cover. Without the storm Lara was not sure they would have made it. The two men disappeared into the trees. She never could see the fire, but she marked the point where they had entered the forest. She ran straight to that foliage.

She could hear men shouting behind her, "Stop, stop. Or we'll shoot."

But she did not stop. She ran harder still.

She heard gunshots fired. She prayed so hard that the bullets would miss. She heard bullets whiz by her head into the forest.

She only had seconds to go until she made it into the woods. The woods in front of her began to change. With only a yard to go, she saw that the place where she was to enter the forest was not a forest really. She could now see the blazing fire. It was a blur otherwise. But she gave one last leap and left Kansas behind.

For a moment, she was floating in whiteness. Her momentum carried her far into oblivion. Finally that sense of being rushed was gone. She was still, and she was safe.

She found herself dry and comfortable. She was sitting in a large cave. There was a bonfire in the center, depressed a few feet in a circular indentation in the floor. And conveniently, there was a hole at the very top of the cavern where all the smoke from the fire emptied into a dark and cold night sky.

"Papa, Raul!" she said with delight. They were safe too. And they were already eating, sitting closer to the fire than she was. They looked up but kept biting into their drumsticks. They had plates on their laps that seemed to be full of green vegetables and biscuits of some sort. And she saw mugs filled with some type of hot beverage by their sides as well.

"Lara, we thought you'd never come," Papa said. She didn't have to guess. She knew that somehow, they had been here much longer than she had. Time was different here. "We're already on our second helping." He smiled from ear to ear.

Lara noticed a man sitting opposite Papa and Raul. He smiled at her. His dress was not modern. She knew instantly that they had gone somewhere back in time. Or should she say somewhen?

"Please, get comfortable. There is a private area in the back there where you can freshen up. We have plenty of time." He smiled. She did not know who this man was, but she decided that she really did need to freshen up.

The area the man had referred to was rather nice. There was a sandy area, well tucked away, that served as a restroom. It was well ventilated and obviously well kept. There was a tiny river where she could take a much-needed sponge bath, and surprisingly, the water temperature was not cold. There were crude but useful instruments to tidy her hair. And there were comfortable clothes laid out for her.

Lara saw her reflection in the pond-like area of the river. The stars and her face made a heavenly portrait. She was struck by the beauty of her surroundings.

When she returned, she saw a plate full of food. It was obviously meant for her, as the men seemed finished with their large meals.

As she was about to be seated, she stole a glance at their mysterious host. He was such a handsome young man. He had a peaceful countenance and seemingly endless patience.

"Professor?" Raul and Papa looked at Lara blankly. But the professor gave Lara an approving nod.

"Are you...Are we...? Professor, where are we?" She was finally able to articulate a simple sentence.

His answer greatly surprised Lara. "Tibet."

Lara's jaw dropped. She had thought Tibet was simply a high plateau. But they were clearly sitting in a large cave. And how in the world did the professor get to Tibet? And why was he so young?

"We are in a sacred place. Tibet has numerous caves, both natural and man made. This cave we are sitting in has been traditionally used as a meditation cave, both in the pre-Buddhist era and post-Buddhism. No one will bother us here."

Lara had many questions, but Professor Oppenheimer motioned for her to eat. The men made satisfactory chitchat while she gathered her strength.

The professor was talking again. "When I saw you in 1965, I was near the end of my life on earth. I did my best, Lara, but you opened my eyes to other dimensions and possibilities. The Creator offered me a job as a mystic traveler. I remembered meeting you. In a way, you are my mentor."

Lara was speechless. He continued.

"I had learned about the human-alien conspiracy. I was trying to help. But, in order to become a mystic traveler, I had to undergo many years of training. From your point of view, I have been training for thousands of years." Lara was stunned.

"Please go on, Professor." He paused to catch his breath.

"But, in any case, I have come to help you in your hour of need. The fire was a test. Raul is saved but he has a different destiny. You, and your Papa here, needed to take that leap of faith." They all sighed. It was a bit of a leap, to say the least.

"No one blames you, Professor. You saved countless people; you helped to end World War II." It was Papa. He knew better than anybody that Hiroshima and Nagasaki were saved as targets by the Allies. There was a military plan all along; the atomic bomb only filled a void that they had already foreseen.

The professor's facial expression was inscrutable. Lara thought she grasped that he was fulfilling his God-given role, that he was doing his best at the time. "Can you tell us what happened?"

"I can do better than that. I can show you." The cave began to disappear, and Lara could perceive they were moving through time.

CHAPTER FORTY-FIVE

MENNONITES

Adam finished stashing all the supplies behind the bushes. He checked his smartphone, and he could see that a severe storm was rolling in. He needed to get back to the hotel as soon as possible. He prayed so hard that Lara was all right, his father too. He kept praying.

"Come on kids, get in the truck," he ordered. They eagerly hopped in. They had had some playtime on the new playground, and they were looking forward to some pool time. It was a good day.

"What about Mommy?" Jacob managed to get that all-important question into the conversation.

"She will meet us at the hotel, Papa too." He smiled reassuringly.

When they got closer to the hotel in Junction City, they could see a large police presence near the hotel. There were some military personnel there as well.

Adam knew it was the human-alien conspiracy finally catching up to him. This was it. Time to go to plan B.

Adam got off at the first stop and made his way across the highway. He was going to have to find an alternative route to Lindsborg. Lara would have to meet them at the castle ruins. That was the meetup spot if ever they were to be separated and their phones did not work.

He drove circuitously to Lindsborg. Instead of going southwest on Highway 70, he went due west on a state road. After a time, he turned left and headed due south to get to Abilene. From there, the highway looked clear once again. He went southwest to Salina. From there, he took Highway 135 due south to Lindsborg.

When the twins had to stop to use the restroom along the way, he noticed an unusually large number of Mennonites standing together in a group in front of the rest area building. They seemed serious and concerned. He had learned about this religious minority population from his wife, who used to work in Newton, a town nearby, and from his priest, who was from Newton. But they were a couple hours north of Newton.

In the 1870s Russian Mennonite settlers began raising Turkey Red hard winter wheat brought from their homeland, and this variety became Kansas's principal agricultural product. Adam recalled that Lara used to muse that Kansas and Ukraine were both the breadbaskets of the world, due in no small part to a common plant, as Ukraine also used the same wheat as its neighboring country of Russia.

Newton was essentially a railroad town, founded in 1871, and it had a mix of religious populations: generally Protestant, but a large population of Catholics as well. There was also this minority of settlers whose beliefs were born out of the sixteenth-century Radical Reformation (which followed the Protestant Reformation). The Mennonites had an almost Amish style of dress. At least the average American might easily confuse the two groups in that regard. The gentlemen wore long beards and donned wide-brimmed hats. The ladies wore long, homemade dresses and simple head coverings.

The Mennonite religion was neither Catholic nor Protestant; it shared beliefs from both groups. Lara had told Adam about them. She had thought, at least superficially, that they were kind of like Episcopalians in that they were in between Catholic and Protestant beliefs, the middle way, as Episcopalians like to phrase it.

But in reality, the Mennonites were markedly different from Episcopalians in their style and culture. And also in their beliefs. Episcopalians were more mainstream, and importantly, Episcopalians did not believe in the need for adult baptism, a repeat baptism because the infant baptism did not count somehow. That was what anabaptism meant, being baptized again as an adult, hence their religious designation of being Anabaptists.

Also Mennonites seemed frozen back in time, not embracing modern styles of dress and conveniences. Although, unlike the Amish, they did not exclude modern conveniences such as phones and cars.

The Mennonites traced their origin to the Swiss Brethren, an Anabaptist group that formed near Zurich on January 21, 1525, facing persecution for their rejection of reformer demands. Ironically, their aim was for religious diversity, and they felt the authorities of the time sought to suppress their movement.

As if on cue, Adam heard one of the men saying something in a whisper. "The police are not helping us. We can't let them take over our homesteads."

Adam's curiosity was piqued. He paused, some feet away from the group, to zip up the twins' jackets. The impending storm, about to strike.

"Where shall we stay? What shall we do?" It was a Mennonite woman.

In a flash, Adam remembered something that Lara had taught him. The Mennonites were pacificists. Perhaps they needed his help.

Adam ushered the boys closer to the group. "Stay by me." To the group, he introduced himself.

"Excuse me, but I could not help but overhear. I'm active military. Can I be of some assistance?" He could see that nearly every face lightened up with hope. He was in the right place at the right time.

He thought of Narada. Or maybe it was Father God, answering his prayers from earlier. Probably the latter. Lord Narada seemed limited to sending him and his wife through time; he was not the one that made the crooked places straight. That was the Creator.

Adam wondered how in the world the Creator managed to get the timing just right. He had thought his plans had been changed at the last minute. It was just a reminder that God was in control, he knew all. Good thing Adam was on God's side.

And then he realized with perfect understanding that God was probably answering the many prayers of this faithful group. God certainly had a knack for getting it right. Adam chuckled. So this is what it is like to live by faith. It is one mystery solved after another. Without end. Love constantly conquering all.

The leader of the group cut Adam's epiphany short. "One of our homes is occupied by a militant, well-armed group. Whenever we try to approach the homestead, dogs come out and bark at us." He pointed to a pregnant woman in the group. Clearly, she and her family needed to get back inside their home.

"The house is well situated, close to the highway, but it also has a small creek running through the property. The land is plentiful. It's idyllic. But Trump supporters can't steal people's property, it's wrong."

Trump supporters? Adam thought fast. "We'll need to give out some firearms. Luckily, I have plenty. I'll show you how to use them. Can we go somewhere to make some plans?"

The men in the group were clearly on board. The women too. The twins heard the conversation, and they trusted their father.

"Daddy, can we help too?" It was Isaiah. Jacob, too, seemed willing to join the fight.

"Maybe," said Adam.

"Probably," he said with a reassuring smile. It was time. Time to be brave, and Adam knew his children were nothing if not brave.

CHAPTER FORTY-SIX

TEST OF FAITH

"There is one other Mennonite house in this area. Let's meet there," the Mennonite leader decided. They all exchanged introductions, and for a moment, the heaviness of their situation seemed lifted. When the owner of that house mentioned that there was plenty of food, the mood further brightened.

The leader's name was Patrick. "How is it that you have so many firearms?" Adam, too, was surprised at his ability to gather so many firearms, with so little notice.

"I asked my comrades if I could borrow their firearms so that I could teach my boys how to clean weapons." It was the truth. He had asked several of his military friends if he might borrow their weapons for this long holiday weekend. They trusted Adam, they knew his family. Getting a little bit of free maintenance on their guns seemed like a good deal, and they could help Adam teach his boys discipline too.

Patrick smiled. "Well, we are glad for your help."

They all gathered at the neighbor's house; they were comfortably inside when the storm struck. There was an ample-sized basement. Safety seemed assured, no matter what the storm could throw at them. There were several young children. Jacob and Isaiah soon made themselves busy playing with all the other children in the large toy area.

"The goal is not to use the firearms, although I do not doubt your bravery and competency. The goal is to oust the intruders from the homestead. But I would also say this: we must thwart their plans to invade more homes and learn of their plans more broadly. This is our chance to observe and learn." The group listened intently to Adam. Their eyes were open wide. It began to dawn on them that this invasion of one home might be part of a bigger plan to do harm to the community at large.

Adam chose a few people to teach about weapons and strategy; he then had each of those leaders take a small group aside and begin teaching them what they had learned from Adam. Soon the house was transformed. What before was idle, excited chatter transitioned into quiet, reverent questioning and study.

Patrick took Adam aside. "Is there something I need to know?" He looked at Adam expectantly.

Adam decided to take a chance. "I know this sounds hard to believe, but there has been a decades-long conspiracy to create chaos in society. I can't go into too many details, but it looks like taking over this home was a strategic move on the conspirators' part. I am guessing that they were counting on little resistance since your faith community is unarmed. The police must be playing some role."

"How could this be? How far does this conspiracy reach?" Those were good questions. Adam wished he could explain everything, but that would take up too much time. And besides, he was pretty sure there was more to the conspiracy than even he and Lara knew about. It was complicated, to say the least.

"My main goal is to help you and the families in your community. But I have to do my part and stop the bad guys. Are you with me?" It was Patrick's turn to reach deep inside of himself. Adam had already resigned himself to this new role weeks ago.

"There is a lab; it has been operational for decades. We believe it was originally located back east, but we have reason to believe that it is now located on the Fort Riley army base. My wife and father are there now. I am pretty sure that they have been captured. If we can get to this lab and destroy it, we should be able to dismantle the conspiracy, at least in large measure. We think there is something in the lab that is controlling people." Adam did not want to mention that it was the very guns that he was providing the Mennonites that were the means for exercising that control.

They were a faithful community. That alone should protect them from the guns' harmful subliminal message. In fact, they might be the only people who could help Adam. It was probably not a coincidence that God had put Adam in league with this group.

"How can using violence prevent violence?" Another good question.

"As I have said, it is not my intention that any of your people should use the firearms, but it is prudent to have guns as protection. These people are dangerous. They won't hesitate to kill even women and children." Patrick nodded his understanding. He sighed.

"We thought that we would be safe here. Kansas is known for its tolerance." Patrick had a sad expression on his face. His people had fled from persecution only to find that their new home was just as oppressive, if not more so.

"It's not oppression against any one group; this conspiracy is actually a method to undermine and destroy all of humanity. Like I said, this is bigger than you and me, for sure." Patrick eyed Adam. He was either out of his mind or he was telling the truth. Everything depended on Patrick at this moment, and somehow, he knew that.

"Join me, Adam, in prayer. It's the only way that we will be successful." They bowed their heads together.

CHAPTER FORTY-SEVEN

HIDDEN BLING BLING

They had a plan. It seemed risky, but it was the only way they could think of. Isaiah and a slender teenage boy from the Mennonite group would enter the homestead down the wooden fire escape and through an unlocked basement window. The family had kept that one window unlocked in order to enter their house or exit it in case of an emergency. The family used the room where that window was located for storage, so they were all hoping that the militiamen would overlook that unlocked window, not bothering to move boxes aside. There was a certain vent in the basement, in that same storage room, where it was possible to hear conversations in the kitchen a floor above. The boys should remain undetected, staying in that one particular room. It was just a matter of getting them through the backyard to that fire escape safely.

The challenge was getting past the dogs. Adam had brought along several cuts of meat. He was envisioning a quiet weekend, hoping against hope that all his preparations were for naught. He could see himself smoking these cuts of meat, he and his father, and his children too, sitting in front of a campfire and enjoying a good old time. Of course he now realized that was a complete fantasy.

But anyway, he had some choice cuts of meat. He couldn't believe he had to give it to strange dogs. If any dog was going to enjoy them, it would be his own precious Mitzie.

"Does anyone have any drugs?" It was a long shot, but hey? Even Mennonites got sick and had orthopedic surgeries. Someone might have some narcotics or barbiturates.

"I do," the slender teenage boy spoke up. Patrick and the other adults looked at him askance.

"Too much to explain. But I have fentanyl and other drugs. The fentanyl will knock the dogs out, if not kill them." The group was in shock, mostly because they knew this young man as a premedical, geeky, and wholesome figure in the community. Was he involved in something nefarious? They were a bit shaken.

"It's not what you think, believe me." But the precocious high school student knew many of his neighbors would never look at him the same. It couldn't be helped. He knew he had to play his role in this effort to take back the homestead. His name was Ryan.

"What do you propose, Ryan?" It was Patrick. Clearly, he was willing to let bygones be bygones, at least for now.

"We stick the fentanyl in each meat package and place it at strategic points along the perimeter of the yard. I think we have counted five dogs in total. It's doable." People were nodding their approval of the plan.

"Who is going to do it?" someone said. Jacob stepped forward.

"I can." It was true. In the family, Jacob was known as the dog whisperer. Sure, it was risky, but he was the best choice. Also, a grown man might be seen as more of a threat by the dogs. Another Mennonite child spoke up. It was a school-aged girl.

"I can help." The Mennonites nodded again. In their community, she was well known for being able to relate to animals. Her name was Emily.

"How is it we are sending children into such dangerous situations?" A woman spoke with caution.

"I know this seems far fetched. But I really think that this can be done. Isaiah and Ryan are just eavesdropping, nothing more. Isaiah is young, but he has a few essential gifts; he has an excellent memory, and he also has a knack for being able to find things. Between him and Ryan in the storage room and Jacob and Emily placating the dogs, we adults should have the opportunity we need to thwart the militia's plans.

"Ryan and Isaiah should be able to get in and out under cover of the storm, especially since the dogs will be out." He and Patrick, and a few other adults, including a few women, would knock out or eliminate any threats from the militiamen on guard, and they would do their best to sabotage the invaders' vehicles. They would have to act fast and with precision.

Everyone was preparing for the attack on the homestead. The storm was growing more and more violent. Weather radios were distributed. Rain gear was donned.

"The main thing is to make it back to the house without being detected. This is our safe place. Use all the precautions we have talked about." The mood was somber. This had to work.

Jacob and Emily left the house first. Emily took the lead. They took their mission very seriously. Jacob was carrying all the meat in a large backpack. He was exceptionally tall and strong for his young age of six; he relished the work. Emily relied on her eye goggles. The wind was whipping in all directions. She knew her landmarks and stuck to her plan.

It took an hour just to get to the other house's fence line. Jacob touched a button on his walkie-talkie. It was the first indication the group in the safe house had that the mission was on track. They were waiting with bated breath for the next signal.

"This fence isn't wired or anything. We can slip through." Sure enough, Jacob could see that she was right. It would be a simple matter for them to crawl into the yard through the fence slats. They could barely hear one another; the wind was that loud. But Jacob knew to start removing the meat packages laced with plenty of fentanyl. These two children could easily relate to one another. Without speaking, they both knew that their goal was not to harm the animals, just to sedate them. They would have to be strategic in how they laid out the meat. Each dog needed their own dose, not double dosing. This was going to take a bit of time.

Jacob handed Emily two packages. She knew this meant that she was to move away from him. They had to spread out so as not to harm the animals and hopefully to drug them all at about the same time. She moved along into the darkest region of the yard; she knew the terrain, Jacob did not.

Emily heard a dog running toward her. Her heart skipped a beat. She laid down one package. She waited for just the right amount of time; luckily, another dog was a bit behind the first. She could time this right. She stealthily moved farther away, and at just the right moment, she placed the second package on the ground. The second dog turned to intercept her. She knelt on the ground in her most welcoming stance, and the dog paused. For a moment, they were looking into each other's eyes.

The dog broke the standoff and chose to pursue the meat, not the little girl. She could breathe again. As the two dogs were eating, she quietly backed away. She was making her way to the area of the fence where she and Jacob had originally entered the yard.

To her great relief, Jacob was already there. "How did you give them the meat so fast?" He put a finger to his lips. She knew she would have to wait to hear about his adventures until they had gotten back to the safe house.

After the requisite twenty minutes, they signaled to the home base that the mission was accomplished. This meant that they could return home.

"I'm going to leave a couple of meat packages here, just in case." She nodded. It was a sound idea. It was difficult for them to ascertain if the dogs had eaten all the meat. Although it certainly seemed like this first part of the attack was going well.

Back at home base, Isaiah and Ryan made their way out into the rain. Ryan took the lead, and Isaiah quietly followed. It was slow going, the wind was fierce.

"Don't top," Isaiah said. Ryan knew that Isaiah was using a special way of talking so that they would not be overheard. He was trying not to use letters like *S*, letters that made sounds that were more easily distinguished among other background noises. Ryan smiled; this kid was smart. Although he thought that the storm precluded the need for such precautions. However, Ryan hastened his pace a bit.

After what seemed a very long time, Isaiah said, "Top." Ryan paused. They crouched down.

"Twin." Ryan was relieved. It was just the other two children; Isaiah had had some sort of sixth sense about his twin being just up ahead. Well, that certainly came in handy.

They all knelt down and hugged one another. They patted each other on the back. It was obvious that

Jacob wanted to stay with his twin and come along for the next adventure. But fortunately, Adam had warned Ryan about that possibility. Jacob was not exactly the quietest person; he was more on the hyper side. If he were to go inside the house, all could be lost.

Ryan put his foot down. He sent Emily and Jacob back to the home base. Disappointed about splitting up, all the children followed the previously decided-upon plan. Jacob was sad, but he took pride in a job well done. No words were spoken, but the storm seemed to punctuate their feelings. It was time to move forward with their plan of action.

Ryan and Jacob gave the signal on their respective walkie-talkies. The adults knew that it was time to move in. Ryan then signaled to Isaiah to follow him. This is where the children would part ways.

They would not be entering the fence line at the same point as the other children had. Ryan was leading them back into a woody area of sorts. It would take them another twenty to thirty minutes to get to the point of the house where the fire escape was located. It was rough going, but Isaiah was used to this type of terrain. It was where he liked to look for frogs and other animals. Besides, he kept his own "pet" frogs in the bottom of their fire escape back home. They never wanted for water and insects to eat. And the frogs were safe from predators. He was looking forward to climbing down into this other fire escape.

Soon the fence line was in front of them. Carefully they made their way through the slats of the fence. Ryan moved across the yard just as they both heard a loud thunderclap. Oh my, Isaiah thought. This is dreadful.

But they made it to the fire escape. This is where Isaiah took over as leader. He was in his element. He lowered himself down into the fire escape and lit a tiny flashlight. Ryan was grateful, climbing trees and the like was not exactly his cup of tea. At least not in recent years. It had been a long time since he had made a habit of climbing trees and playgrounds. Thank goodness he could see the ladder more clearly now.

Just as Ryan alighted from the ladder, Isaiah put his fingers to his lips and pointed to the window. It was Ryan's turn to act; he gently tried to open the window. They held their breath. Would it work? Would it open? They had taken such pains to get here.

And then with a final nudge, Ryan pried it open. It worked!

Isaiah trusted the plan; he moved in first. It was a small area between the window and the boxes, but he made it. He pushed just a tiny bit with his body and made room for the larger boy. They had both popped into the room without incident or injury.

Ryan shut the window. It was like heaven shutting out the thunderous noise of the endless rain. It was quiet as a tomb in the storage room. And dark too.

They just sat there, listening. Soon they heard what were like voices from overhead; the conversation was coming from the vents. They dared not speak to one another. If they could hear the voices through the vent, then that meant it was possible for the other occupants of the house to hear them as well. They sat down and got comfortable. Ryan clicked the record button on his phone. They leaned toward the vent.

"She won't make it. But just in case." It was a man's voice. He had an accent that was strange to the two boys.

"Where did you hide it?" It was another man's voice.

But that was all that the two boys could understand really. The conversation was not interesting to them. Time passed, and still they went undetected in the house. The storm outside raged on.

Ryan signaled to Isaiah to follow him. Isaiah was too scared to move. He dared not leave this storage room. But Ryan knew that his friend's house had an adjacent family room where there was a games closet. He really wanted to get one of those board games. He could slip it into his backpack, and no one upstairs would be the wiser.

Ryan shrugged. It did not matter to him if Isaiah followed or not. He would be right back. Isaiah left the phone near the vent, still recording, and followed Ryan. Just as Ryan remembered, there was a closet door off the main room. All was dark and quiet. He gently opened the door.

Isaiah turned on his tiny flashlight. If he was going to veer off course, he might as well help Ryan. As he was looking for his game, Isaiah was scanning the floor of the closet. He felt sure that he had seen a tiny glow of light coming out from underneath the bottom shelf of the closet. He knelt down and stuck his head under the lowest shelf. In the back corner there was a tiny box, the size of a box that might hold a wedding ring or something special along those lines. He shivered with excitement. What a find.

Ryan nudged Isaiah's feet. Clearly, he had found his all-important game. Isaiah decided to open the glowing box. His eyes lit up with astonishment. Inside the box was the most beautiful stone that he had ever seen, and it generated its own light. How fascinating.

Well, might he add this stone to his collection? What could be the harm in bringing it back to his father and the Mennonites? The worst that could happen is that they would tell him that he could not keep it.

So he stashed the stone in his pocket. Just as he was moving back into the room, he accidentally bumped Ryan and his body made one of the games on the upper shelf fall to the floor.

Damn, thought Ryan. He placed the fallen game back into its proper place in the closet. They returned to the storage room and hid behind some boxes after Ryan hastily powered down the smartphone. It was only a minute later that the storage room door opened, and a strong beam of light flashed across the room.

Ryan and Isaiah lay still as rocks, their hearts pounding. Finally, the door closed. It was dark once again. Their plan had worked. It was time to go out into the storm and make their way home.

Now that Isaiah had found this unexpected bling in the house, this glowing stone, he was even more hopeful that he might find a frog in the fire escape and bring it home as well. Maybe Dad would let him keep it as a pet?

As Ryan was closing the window behind them, Isaiah shone his light on the ground of the fire escape. With practiced ease, he recognized two eyes peering through the sand. The frog was buried, all except his eyes. Isaiah was elated; he quickly dug it out and placed it into his backpack. Ryan signaled for Isaiah to turn the light off. They climbed out of the fire escape and back into the dark wind howling all around them. Ryan was thinking of a hearty meal such as a pot roast dinner. Isaiah was thinking of making a habitat for his new pet.

They lumbered home, their mission accomplished and then some.

CHAPTER FORTY-EIGHT

FLEEING FOR THEIR LIVES

The rainstorm had turned into a full-blown thunderstorm. Thank goodness the children were back at the safe house. But where were the adults? Isaiah and Jacob were worried about their dad. But they knew that he could take care of himself.

They were exhausted. They had had a great adventure out in the rain, their respective tasks completed, but it would be nearly impossible to wait up for the attack party. Besides, there were plenty of adults back home here, and the mothers especially were encouraging all the children to get ready for bed.

Brushing their teeth, petting and playing with Mitzie and the other dogs—it was a bit of a ruckus to be sure. Soon the yawns were too pronounced to ignore.

Sleeping bags and blankets were laid out on the family room floor. The lights were dimmed. All the kids were still managing to ask Isaiah, Jacob, Emily, and Ryan about their exploits.

"Shh. Go to sleep. All is well. Praise be to God." It was Ryan. He was a voice of authority and somehow all the kids knew that they needed to listen to him.

"Praise be to God," they all chimed in. "Amen." There were a few children squirming and giggling, but then all fell silent. They were fast asleep.

In the morning, a ray of sunshine was visible on the floor. It was crossing over one of the children's eyes. Its warmth was welcome. The children woke up cozily and with excitement. Everyone wanted to hear what had happened last night.

Isaiah and Jacob ran up the stairs, Ryan and Emily following close behind. They popped into the kitchen and found that the attack party was not present. The adults in the room looked somber.

"What happened?" Jacob was stricken. He was always deeply affected when other people got hurt.

"Patrick got injured. I'm afraid it is pretty bad. He lost a lot of blood. But he and the others are sleeping comfortably right now. Let's pray for his speedy recovery." It was a kindly woman. Jacob liked her most of all. They hugged one another. Everyone bowed their heads and prayed.

"Did anyone analyze the recording that we made? What happened with the adults?" Ryan was eager to find out when the homestead would be liberated and how that would be done.

"Good morning." Adam came bounding out of his room. The twins were elated to see him and ran to his arms.

"We've arranged to drive Patrick to the emergency room in Newton. They will check his blood level, and if he needs a transfusion or any surgery, then he will get the best of care. He will recover well." The group let out a collective sigh of relief. Patrick was their rock.

Adam knew that they wanted more of an explanation. So, he began to give them all a blow by blow over a hearty breakfast.

"We received all the prearranged signals, good job kids!" The four beamed with pride.

"We had to act fast because the rain and windstorm were turning into a full-blown thunderstorm. Pretty much at the same time that Ryan and Isaiah were in the storage room, we adults had just arrived to the fence line. No dogs came to greet us. We were happy about the wooden fence. We tried our best to mitigate any lightning strikes." The mood was almost jovial as they heard the amazing story of the adults.

The family who owned the homestead was on the edge of their seats.

"We had on our face coverings and nondescript gear. I don't think our identities were ever detected. That is a blessing. But please be ready today. We may need to make a fast exit if for some reason they find out that we were responsible for the damage to their vehicles."

"Damage? What kind of damage?" All the kids wanted to know, and the other members of the group too.

"We came across several militiamen. Some of us made a commotion away from the driveway; they followed us. It was dark and the wind was blowing. We stopped in an area of the yard where the moonlight could not reach. As we crouched down low, we spaced out, waiting to pounce once the men came within reach."

They listened intently.

"Just as they were about to reach us, close enough that they could shoot us, one of us made a sound about a stone's throw away. Sure enough, the militiamen let loose with their gunfire. We had wire loops that we quickly used to wrap around their ankles and pull tight in order to make them fall. It was a major struggle, wrestling the firearms away from these men. But by the grace of God, no one was shot."

"Whew," someone in the group said.

"Thanks be to God," said another.

"We did have to knock a few of them out, but we managed to get them all tied with their hands behind their backs."

Adam went on to explain that they brought back all of the firearms and ammunition that they could carry. The people in charge of disabling the vehicles did a good job. All the tires, including the spares, were slashed. It was hard work in the rain.

"But soon, we ran out of time. The militiamen in the house were alerted by the gunshots, they regrouped, and we would have been injured, if not captured, if we had not run away."

"Then how did poor Patrick get hurt?" Ryan asked.

It was then that one of the bedroom doors opened, and out came Patrick. He was bandaged in his midriff and walking slowly. He looked a bit pale, but it seemed his spirits were not dashed.

"I thought I was in Jesus's tomb for a moment there, it was so dark and gruesome. These bandages sure didn't help." A few of the women laughed. They could see where it being Easter morning and all, the many wraps that they had put around him did indeed make him look a little like the risen Christ.

"I fell on the fence while I was trying to jump over it. I think the fence caught my spleen or something." A man was waiting at the door.

"It's time, Patrick. Let's go." He acquiesced; he was ready to go to the hospital. But, although he had had a close call, he had never felt more alive. Deep down he knew that what they had accomplished that night was significant, thanks mostly to Adam and his family.

"This means a lot to our group, Adam, your help and support. We never could have achieved so much without your help. I only wish that I could be with you to finish the job." Adam smiled. And the injured leader and his ride left for the hospital.

The mood brightened. Now they took to discussing their next move. But they had a moment for levity, and the children took advantage of the break. The sun was shining, and the spring day was warmer than the days prior.

They had just finished a morning snack and break when someone heard some noises outside.

"It sounds like a caravan is coming this way." A few of them used binoculars at the windows. They saw numerous pickup trucks with large, waving American flags.

"It's the militiamen!"

Adam made the dreaded sign for everyone to bug out. Armed with knives and firearms, they all hurriedly got into the vehicles that were equipped for off-roading. Rather than driving on the roads, as the militiamen might expect them to do, they drove over the farmland, a predetermined plan to take the fastest route to Coronado Heights Castle in Saline County.

Isaiah was among the group getting in the family's truck, along with Mitzie. "How could they find us?" He was worried that they might be missing their stone. It took him a moment, but he began to put two and two together. That man with the accent had hidden something, and somehow Isaiah knew that he had been the one to find that hidden object. He must tell dad about this.

"Daddy, I have something that they want." Adam was perplexed. But knowing Isaiah, he quickly turned his attention to his son. Albeit with some spotty concentration on his part, since he was driving at top speed over bumpy cornfields.

"What happened in that storage room?" Isaiah told his story, including the part about finding a new "pet" frog at the end.

"Isaiah, you should have told me that right away." Adam saw his crestfallen face.

"It's not your fault, son. Not at all. And of course you can keep that frog." Isaiah's face brightened.

"But you had better put that stone in the locked armrest compartment." He did as he was told. He was so relieved that his dad was not angry with him. Instead he seemed almost proud. Isaiah knew somehow that he had done good. Although he had no idea how it could be good that they were fleeing for their lives.

After some time, the group lost the militiamen that had been in pursuit. They drove up to some hackberry trees that lined the border between two farms. Everyone opened their windows.

"Do whatever it takes to get to the castle. We will set up camp at the top of the hill." All the vehicles drove off. Traffic was practically nonexistent since it was a holiday. They drove as if their lives depended on it.

CHAPTER FORTY-NINE

THE TRUE FORM OF GOD

Professor Oppenheimer led them to an ancient battlefield. They were in India. Lara knew it right away. Papa and Raul were still confused; they remained silent, observing their surroundings. Gone was the comforting cave in Tibet.

The four of them hovered at a distance. They could see multiple factions about to fight it out.

"What is happening?" asked Lara.

"The royal lineage has come into conflict. Two sets of cousins each believe that they are the rightful heirs. On one side are five brothers. On the other, a hundred sons of a blind regent." They all nodded for the professor to go on.

"The third Pandava brother, Arjuna, and his brothers have some special help. See Arjuna, there in the chariot? See his companion?" They did see. There was a beautifully ornate chariot, and inside were two men.

They were dazzling in their splendor. And so was the entire battlefield, for that matter.

They saw elephants draped in gold and armor glittering with gems. There were flags of all colors, battle standards indicating might. The countryside was fresh and green with fervent life. The air was the sweetest that any of the modern observers had ever experienced. The world was a different place thousands of years ago, it was like new.

Yet here in front of them were the familiar conflicts that the three of them had always learned about in school. Family fighting family. A community fighting within itself.

The professor indicated for them to listen. Somehow, although they were a few hundred yards away, Papa, Lara, and Raul could overhear what the prince was saying.

"I do not see foot soldiers and archers. I do not see charioteers. I see fathers, grandfathers, teachers, sons, and friends." He looked at his companion, not yet realizing that he was speaking to the god Krishna in disguise. His knees were weak, he was shaking from dread. He could not go on. He dropped his weapons.

Krishna revealed himself, and he was laughing; Arjuna was weeping.

Krishna said, "This is precisely why you have been brought to this moment. To understand that the divine self can never die. If you slay your family, their essence will live on." Arjuna was listening but far from understanding. Krishna went on, teaching and guiding him.

"Professor, can the others see and hear us?" Lara said. They were removed from the battlefield, but to Lara they were somehow part of it. They should not have been able to hear the conversation between the two warriors, Krishna and Arjuna, but nevertheless they could hear it. The professor nodded in the affirmative.

"Don't they think it strange that we are here?" Lara wondered.

"This battlefield is more than just a reflection of human beings fighting for a throne. Arjuna himself is related to the god Krishna." Papa, Raul, and Lara opened their mouths in wonder. To them, that would be like saying that one of the Christian saints was related to Jesus, and that cannot be.

"In the Bhagavad Gita, the story of divine and mortal beings intermingling is very complex." Lara could see that the professor was more than interested in this part of the epic tale of Hindu mythology. He was somehow a part of it.

"Professor, are you that human prince? Are you Arjuna?" She could see it now. There was a resemblance between them; it was far fetched, but somehow Lara saw a connection. She saw that there might be multiple reasons that the professor had brought them all here.

"Lara, I can never hide anything from you. Yes, you have grasped the truth. My destiny is to be tested; I had to learn to play my role and execute my duty. I had to learn." Lara felt compassion for the professor. She could barely understand how this Krishna and human prince story related to her current life; she had little to no understanding of the Hindu gods. But clearly, the professor was showing her and her companions something of importance here. They, too, had to learn.

"Sh. Listen," said Raul.

It felt as though time had stopped. Krishna had been teaching Arjuna for what seemed a very long time. Arjuna was beginning to see that in this moment he was more than just a warrior. He was fulfilling his role in the entire universe. He had to learn about his true nature, his divine origin.

Arjuna began to grasp that Krishna was part of the true form of God. Arjuna was no longer just a warrior struggling with his duty to fight his brethren; he was transcending, he was breaking free from his karma, turning toward Vishnu, the true God.

"Please show me your true, immortal self, the master of all creation," he begged.

Krishna grants Arjuna spiritual sight because human eyes cannot perceive the truth of God. With this ability, Arjuna then sees, and Lara's group also saw, the true form of God. The battlefield was forgotten. They saw a being who shone like a thousand suns all rising together. Krishna's true self has an infinite number of faces overseeing the entire universe. Lara thought she saw Sujita's face.

Krishna carried countless weapons in countless hands as symbols of his limitless power.

They saw Krishna, and his form was the form of every object that has ever existed merged into one.

Arjuna fell to his knees. Lara and her group genuflected as well. They saw Brahma, Father God, as Lara knew him. He was sitting on a lotus flower, his warmth radiating and shining light on everything that exists.

Arjuna was overcome, but he managed to inquire, to beg, asking Vishnu to explain what he was.

"I am time, the ultimate destroyer. Everyone gathered at this battlefield will die eventually. No matter what you do, that fact will not change. Therefore, you must fulfill your dharma and lead the Pandavas into battle."

"Dharma?" Papa asked. He knew next to nothing about Hinduism. He was trying his best to follow along.

"The eternal and inherent nature of reality, regarded in Hinduism as a cosmic law underlying right behavior and social order," the professor explained.

"Are you saying, Professor, that you had to play your part in being the father of the atomic bomb?" Lara barely understood what this revelation meant, the big leap of understanding that she might be making. She could only just grasp that it meant that there was an urgency to being saved. At least, that is how she saw it. She could see that in the Hindu religion, it was similar;

only if you could transcend karma and reincarnation would you be free to rejoin with God. Like Sujita had.

It was all one big test. And Lara felt like she was barely passing.

"What came first? The Indian human prince story or your story as Professor Oppenheimer?" Lara offered. She realized that to think in linear terms was somewhat restrictive. Maybe the professor's story was more convoluted than she thought.

"Exactly," he answered. At that, Lara had had enough. She felt like her brain was going to explode. She looked at Raul and he appeared extremely sleepy. Papa, well, he looked something like a madman, about to be undone.

The air around them began to swirl in whiteness. "Wait! Please, Professor, don't go. Please tell me, what does all this have to do with the human-alien conspiracy?" she shouted.

"You are the warrior, Lara. You are the human prince now. It's time." She saw a tear in his eye, and with that he disappeared.

For a long time, Lara and the others were floating in that in-between place; she was weeping uncontrollably, not knowing why. But soon she felt a spiritual hug from every angle, and her confusion and sadness turned to comfort and peace. She fell asleep, a deep sleep that rejuvenated her completely.

There was no way to know how long she and the others had been sleeping. But, at some point, they woke up. And they realized that they were being drenched by the rain. They were right back where they had started, on the edge of that big field where the bad guys had been chasing them.

CHAPTER FIFTY

DO OR DIE

"Lara, what the heck was all that?" Papa said.

"All what?" She barely wanted to talk about it. About anything.

"We're being drenched here. Let's find that lab you talked about." It was Raul.

Thank God Raul had the presence of mind to say something practical. It was what they all needed. A purpose. Not the purpose, but a purpose. It was the best that they could do in that moment.

"Can you lead us back? And where are all the bad guys?" They looked around. Lara and the others saw no one, no one at all. It felt like the army base was deserted.

"Yes. Let's get our gear." They saw all of their supplies strewn around them. Thankfully, they were wearing their new clothes from the Tibetan cave. But what good were the new outfits if they got soaking wet?

They donned some rain gear and hastily ate a few bites. Grateful for attending to some basic needs, not having to ponder what it means to leave time and this world behind. The lab. They had to switch their focus to the lab.

They retraced their steps, not bothering to pause at the playground, moving stealthily along to their destination. To their surprise, the building with the supposed lab in it had been destroyed. It had been blown to smithereens.

"What the..." Papa was saying when they saw some soldiers off in the distance.

"Quick, let's get out of here," Lara said. They made their way back to the truck. It was still parked in the same spot in front of the fitness center.

Papa was driving with Lara and Raul guiding him. She knew that their ultimate destination was the castle ruins in Lindsborg. But Raul knew better than anyone how to get off the army base. He guided them to an exit, one that was hardly used.

"This is no time to obey traffic signals, Papa. Let's just get out of here." Papa didn't need any encouragement to hit the pedal to the metal. He took their escape to a new level: he veered off the road and he put the truck into four-wheel drive.

Mud splattered everywhere. Behind them they could see multiple government vehicles in pursuit. Thank God Lara and Papa had filled their tank with gas before they had gone to the gym. They should be able to make it to the castle, as long as no one tried to intercept them on the way.

It was a long and harrowing journey; Lara was able to explain that meeting at the castle ruins was their last resort. She didn't have any plan after they met up with her family. They sobered at the thought.

Raul was listening to the radio and trying to get a signal on his smartphone. As Papa drove over obstacle after obstacle, the truck swerving and tilting in response to his fast speed, he listened with astonishment as Raul filled them in on the news.

Apparently an armed group of militiamen had stormed the capitol building in Topeka. A civil war had broken out. National Guardsmen had been called, but at the capitol building, even some military and police personnel seemed to be on the side of the bad guys. Ordinary citizens were outgunned and outmanned. It was a massacre.

Raul let out an agonizing groan. "What is it?" Lara asked with fear.

"All fifty state capitols have been attacked. It's the second civil war in the United States, starting today!" Papa drove faster. He was crazed with anger. Anger toward the bad guys, but also anger toward himself for coming to a deeper spiritual understanding late in the game, maybe too late.

All Lara could do was pray. She hoped her family was all right. She wanted to hug Adam and her kids. She wanted everything to go back to normal. But it was then that she realized that the only normal worth wishing for was to be one with God. That was what God was trying to tell her, and everyone really: through it all, the only thing that could really make you feel at peace was to be in union with God. Everything else was only approaching happiness, everything else was like a shadow of the true sun that was God.

Lara felt peace come over her being. It would be all right now. She was in the right place, at the right time. It was meant to be.

"What the..." It was Papa again. He sure had excellent vision, thought Lara. They all saw it. It was Adam and the boys driving their other truck. And there were other vehicles alongside him, driving like the wind.

"Raul, give me that walkie-talkie!" He immediately reached for it in the back seat and handed it to Lara in the front passenger seat.

"Mama Bear here, this is Mama Bear, over." They waited.

She said it again, "This is Mama Bear. Over." They heard a response.

"Mama Bear, this is Baby Cub and Baby Cub, over." They cheered. Lara cried.

"Bad guys in pursuit, use all caution. Over," she said.

"Message received. Understood. Same here. Over." Oh no, thought Lara. This was not looking good.

Lara did not know what to say. Her mind was a blank. "Hold the walkie-talkie to my mouth, Lara," said Papa.

"This is Papa Bear. This is Papa Bear. We're going to be okay. Over." How he knew that was a mystery, but it sure made their hearts beat a bit slower to be reassured.

"Papa, Papa." It was Isaiah. And he had forgotten to say "over."

No one else spoke again. All they could do was keep driving now. It was do-or-die time. And everyone dies eventually, thought Lara, isn't that what Vishnu had said? But she was a mystic traveler; she had learned to travel through time. Time may be running out, but she had a few tricks up her sleeve. She was not about to give up, not yet.

CHAPTER FIFTY-ONE

CONFESSION OF A SAINT

They all skidded to a stop, throwing up mud and debris. As if in unison, they departed from their vehicles and began unpacking necessary gear. Everyone took all that they could carry and rapidly hiked up the three-hundred-foot hill to the castle ruins called Coronado Heights.

The sun was shining; it was a beautiful day, finally. The clouds had all disappeared. If it had been any other Easter day, the deeply religious group would have seen the change in weather as providential. As it was, they were just grateful to be relieved of the pounding rain in their faces. They raced to set up camp, to find positions inside the castle and at the perimeter of the peak that were most strategic in defending their little mountain. A few people had time to race back down to the vehicles and retrieve more supplies. Isaiah was among them. Without being told, he unlocked the truck compartment that held the stolen stone, and he hid the stone in one of his pants pockets.

"Come on," someone yelled.

Everybody looked at the horizon. Sure enough, there were countless all-terrain vehicles heading their way.

"Run!" somebody else yelled.

Isaiah ran with all of his might. He was lagging behind the grown men, laden down with a few more choice items. He had gone back for his precious backpack, the one that held all his favorite dinosaurs and airplanes. He couldn't let the bad guys get them.

Isaiah reached the peak and ran into his mother's arms just as the army vehicles crashed into their parked cars at the foot of the hill. Good thing I got my stuff, thought Isaiah.

Adam and Lara hugged. The Mennonites, too, were rejoicing that they had made it this far. But their victory of escape was short lived. Adam was yelling orders now.

"To arms, to arms. Everyone, find your spot. This is it!" Adam had delegated duties to all, even the children. There would be some people solely responsible for firing guns and some people to administer water and give aid if needed. There were some people in charge of replenishing ammunition.

A shot was fired; it had come from down below. The castle had been hit. Soon the entire area was crashing with gunfire. Some of the troops were headed up the hill. One by one, their group fell from being shot. Adam's family and the Mennonites fought for their lives. Each man, woman, and child gave their all. But it was no use. It was only a matter of time; they were outgunned and outmanned.

The militiamen were accompanied by police officers as well. There seemed to be regular citizens in their group too. All seemed lost.

There was a slight pause in the cadence of the fighting. They all heard a man's voice shout, "Stop. We need to find the stone."

Lara looked at Adam. He read her mind. She was wondering what this stone was that the man was referring to. He gave her a look. She instantly knew that he had found it. Or someone had. And she knew that it was important.

"Get her," the same man said. Out of the nearby trees some men leaped out; they overcame Lara and held her by all her limbs. She was powerless as she stood there in a position as if about to be quartered.

"Stop," Adam yelled.

The Mennonites obeyed. Both sides were still. It was clear to all that this moment was pivotal. Out of the same trees and from out behind the castle, some of the same aliens that had captured Lara and Papa popped out into the middle of the crowd. The Mennonites gaped. The soldiers looked worried.

Parker stepped forward. "We know you have it, Lara. Give it up, and your death will be quick. And your family's too."

"Pray," she yelled. The Mennonites needed no such urging. Everyone kneeled in prayer. Someone started chanting the Lord's Prayer, and soon all the good guys joined in.

Out of nowhere, Kunal and the assassin lady came into view. The agent, too, appeared on the scene.

"Lara, fancy meeting you here." It was Kunal.

Lara replied with a grunt. She resumed praying.

Some soldiers were making their way up the hill, and among them was Pavan. He came forward like a bad wind, about to blow with anger.

Parker spoke again, "So, it comes to this. I didn't think you would make it this far, Lara. You have my respect."

Lara could see that they were outnumbered. But all was not lost. The bad guys didn't have the stone, whatever that was. It was subtle, but she saw her son Isaiah squirm. Unconsciously, he was reaching into his left pants pocket.

He has it, thought Lara. Well, there was no way in hell that she was going to let her son Isaiah be manhandled by these goons.

"Isaiah, remember the popcorn game?" He was relieved to hear his mother speak. He knew what she wanted. He was a great aim, and she was great at catching the popcorn in her mouth. He took the stone out of his pocket and aimed for his mommy's mouth.

It happened so fast; the men couldn't stop what was happening. Lara swallowed the stone. It was large, but she gulped hard. Too late, bastards, I have it now, and you're not getting it, she thought.

"Give me that stone," Parker said.

"Over my dead body," she said with equal command.

It was a standoff. "We can make that happen," said Parker.

But before he could act, Pavan grabbed Isaiah. The assassin lady grabbed Jacob. The agent had a plan. He stepped forward.

"You never cease to surprise me, Lara. You've opened my eyes to other dimensions, other possibilities. For that I thank you. But it doesn't change the fact that I need my stone." Everyone's eyes gazed at the agent. He seemed to be steaming, literally. The aliens perked up at that statement. Until now, they had been observers. Now one of them spoke. He was using some sort of translating device.

"Your stone? Do you forget yourself?" he spoke with deadly finality. It was a thinly veiled threat.

But the agent was going rogue. He now knew more about what was at stake. He had the power to travel to other worlds, perhaps more so than these pesky aliens. All he needed was that stone. Then he could begin to control other worlds. It was the weapon that he desired.

And he would take Kunal and the assassin lady with him. And Pavan too, if he had any sense left in that harebrained head of his.

Parker gave a slight nod, and the military men under his command came to attention, their guns cocked. Lara realized something. What was once a lab must have been chiseled down into this stone, metaphor intended, infused with alien technology; it was what everybody wanted. She realized that it must hold the power to control the guns made by the military-industrial complex. If she could destroy the stone, then probably she could free the world from the human-alien conspiracy's vicelike grip. And probably this catastrophic civil war would end.

There was still hope. She also realized that she had a little leverage. As long as the stone was in her belly, she had a slight advantage. By now all the bad guys knew she had the power to travel through time.

Kunal took a rifle and aimed it at Adam. "We have your family, Lara. What's it going to be?"

She was a fool. She had no leverage. It was her family or the stone. Even worse, even if she gave either set of bad guys the stone, there was no guarantee that her family would be spared. Or herself for that matter.

It was an impossible situation.

She smiled. Papa smiled. They both knew there was hope.

"Jesus Christ is the Lord and Savior of the world," she said simply. If all was lost, then she and the other believers in the crowd would be saved. Their essence would live on, they would have a chance to join with God, and in the end, that was all that mattered.

"No!" yelled Kunal. He had been banished from that in-between place, and now he knew that he would be banished from earth. Lara had said the one thing that he and the other bad guys could never say. And he knew that they would pay a price for their unbelief.

The wind picked up; a rainbow glistened in the sky. As everyone was looking up at the spectacle of color newly formed in the heavens above, the wind swooped up the agent and his minions. As Kunal was blowing away into oblivion, he shouted, "I'll get you for this, Lara!" And he was gone.

But Pavan remained. He was kneeling on the ground praying. He was overcome by the rainbow. He remembered that his sister, Sujita, had been with God when he had ordered that his parents be sent to India, and surely, this rainbow was her doing.

As for the other bad guys, many of them dropped their weapons in confusion. There was a general pause and Adam took advantage of it.

"Take their firearms and tie them up." The Mennonites worked fast and began rounding up the soldiers who had been with Parker. Parker himself was detained by a Mennonite, and he glared as his hands and feet were bound.

The aliens looked at Lara and her family. "You've won, Lara. It's over. But we will be back for that stone.

When it's time." She could almost imagine that the alien had chuckled when he said it. But she couldn't be sure through the translation device.

"Don't be late. Time is always running out." And as she said that, the aliens disappeared into thin air.

CHAPTER FIFTY-TWO

GHOST STORIES

Mrs. Patel called Lara. After exchanging pleasantries, she said, "I am sorry I am just calling now. I had a strange experience at the Singapore airport, and I needed time..." She broke off. Obviously, whatever had happened to her there had been life changing.

"It's okay, Mrs. Patel. No worries. I have news about Pavan though." The long-suffering mother made a sound as if to say something in response, but then she stopped herself.

"But first, I have to tell you something." There was a long pause. Lara waited.

"I know this is hard to believe, but..." Still, she hesitated.

"Mrs. Patel, you can tell me anything," Lara reassured.

"Okay. I will just say it then. God told me to warn you. It's a trap or something. Something about a lab." Lara smiled. Everyone is on their own path, at their own pace. Including Mrs. Patel.

"Don't worry, Mrs. Patel. I know. Thanks for thinking of me, though." Lara could hear a sigh of relief on the other end of the phone. Mrs. Patel had done what she was supposed to do. Lara laughed inside, knowing that Mrs. Patel could learn a thing or two about timing.

"Is there anything else you need to tell me?" Somehow Lara knew that there was more to the story.

"No. At least, not what I am comfortable sharing at this time. Maybe later." She was still in shock from her mystical experience, Lara knew it had to be that.

"Of course. When it's the right time, you'll know." Mrs. Patel agreed. They would talk about it again when she was ready.

"What did you want to tell me about Pavan?" Lara was glad to shift to a subject that Mrs. Patel *was* ready for.

"He had a change of heart. He wants to come home." Mrs. Patel was all happiness.

Lara filled her in. Pavan was found guilty of seditious conspiracy against the United States government. He and others had planned an insurrection, and he had been caught on tape planning the crime. But because he was fully cooperating, he had only gotten six months of probation. He had to stay in Kansas for those entire six months, but once he was released, he planned to reunite with family permanently.

Mrs. Patel was beside herself with joy. "Oh, Lara. You have made me the happiest woman alive. I prayed so hard that he would turn. Actually, when God spoke to me in the airport, I think he was answering my prayer about his salvation." She couldn't speak any more. She was elated.

They hung up, both satisfied with the call. Lara knew that it was just a matter of time; one day, she would be able to tell Mrs. Patel the whole story. One day.

But then she realized that probably it would be Pavan to tell her the story. And that was probably for the best. It was meant to be.

She told Adam about the call. He laughed, "Well, that would have been helpful to know. Ahead of time." And then Lara and Adam were both laughing. It was all about time after all.

The phone rang. It was Sujata. "My mom told me. What happened?" So Lara began to tell Sujata everything.

"Then what happened?" she said, eager to hear the rest of the story after Lara had swallowed the stone, after she had prayed about Jesus.

Lara explained that once the aliens disappeared, the Mennonites and Adam pretty much had things in hand. But it was unclear where to put the criminals or who to call.

But then coming up the hill was Fred, the police officer that had helped her find the key to the conspiracy. He had given her access to the mass shooting crime scene, and that is how Lara had found out about the subliminal message.

Adam had filled him in. Then Ryan, one of the Mennonite kids, had thrown the tape into Fred's hands. He had said, "This is what you need. It's all there."

"Wow," said Sujata.

She then explained to Lara that she had seen on the news that the United States had had an insurrection, but that it had been quelled. It seemed that that event had shocked the nation and the crime rate had gone plummeting down. But it was not only the United States. Almost the entire world seemed to be experiencing a sudden decrease in violence. Of all sorts. Even the Russians were pulling out of Ukraine. No one knew why Putin had changed his mind.

"But I digress, then what happened?" Sujata begged for more.

Lara explained that several of the religious group had been shot and wounded. But strangely, they could not find a single casualty. Emily, the young girl that had helped to drug the dogs, had bright red blood all over her clothes, but not a single wound.

"No." Sujata was incredulous.

"Yes. In fact, there was not a single casualty or wound. Ambulances had been dispatched to the scene, and they could not find anyone to treat." Lara herself was trying to take it all in. But she was comfortable enough with what had happened to talk about it. Actually, telling the story out loud to her friend really helped her realize exactly what had happened.

"Lara, it was a miracle. And you are the saint who performed it!"

"With God's help," Lara answered. But she knew it was more than that.

"And not to mention all the believers who were there: Papa, the guard Raul, my beloved Adam, Isaiah and Jacob, and who could forget the incredible Mennonites. It was a group effort." And God had rewarded that effort. He had saved the world, she thought.

And she could not leave out Lord Narada and Aravia too. She told Sujata her thoughts. She could not quite process her experiences with Professor Oppenheimer yet, so she kept those to herself.

"Thanks be to the gods," Sujata said.

This time it was Lara that was quiet. She understood Mrs. Patel's reticence only too well. Some things are hard to process and difficult to talk about. Even for Lara.

They promised to talk again, and then hung up. Sujata was eager to hear from her brother. She would reach out with the contact information that Lara had provided.

Lara left her bedroom to join the rest of the family in the living room. They were all going camping at El Dorado Lake, not too far from home. It was their second spring break, and they needed a true rest. It had been a busy school year. It was time to enjoy the here and now. Time for cooking by the campfire and telling ghost stories. Only this time, they might add in an alien or two.

"Yep," Adam said.

"And now that the stone is out of your body, we might just see one or two." They all laughed, not scared at all.

Lara looked down at the stone in her hands. It was dull. Isaiah had said that it was giving off some light. Maybe somehow the aliens had turned it off. For whatever reason, the aliens had changed their minds. They had said it was over, and they were right. Lara thought about her friend in time, Professor Oppenheimer.

Lara spoke softly so that no one else in the room could hear. "Thanks, Professor. You were the father of the atomic bomb. And now, you are the mystic traveler that helped to save the world. We'll meet again. It's just a matter of time." And then she went to hug her husband. It would be a good day.

THE END